What People are Saying about

"A must-read. Gripping and captivating, very well written. Excellent plotting with enough embedded twists to keep readers on the edge to the end. I was sold on it from the get go, this book will make a great movie."

~Phillip B. Goldfine
Film, Television & Broadway Producer

"*Seven Roses* is truly one of a kind. It's very rare to find such an unpredictable and engaging story that continually keeps you guessing, and I guarantee that you won't be able to put it down. With everything from romance and unconditional friendship, to mystery and thrilling twists and turns, this book will have you on the edge of your seat until the very end."

~ Michelle Sugar, PhD, Classics; Published Author

"*Seven Roses* is the most extraordinary book I have ever read! I literally couldn't put it down. It is a true page-turner. Be prepared to be captivated and ensure you block off plenty of time to read the entire book in one sitting as you won't want to stop reading. It's gripping, engaging and shocking! I love this book and I believe you will as well."

~ Peggy McColl, *New York Times* Best-Selling Author

"I LOVED *Seven Roses*. The prose was really evocative and made me cry several times—perfect! The characters all had depth and it was a pleasure to witness the synchronicities unfold. This story is a great example of the Universe being in alignment and everything happening for a reason. The plot was well-conceived and flowed. I couldn't stop reading! I can't wait to see what Ms. Tremblay writes next."

~ Corinne L. Casazza, best-selling author of *Walk Like an Egyptian* and *The Adventures of Blue Belly and Sugar Shaker*.

"As I'm writing this testimonial outside in my backyard, a butterfly fluttered around my face…

A mystical book that hooks you on the first page and you don't want to put it down. The writing is inspiring; it reveals insight that comes from perception and growth that emerges from grief. As a woman, I believe that secrecy is the price to pay for your past. But this book is a powerful story of triumph which lights the way to healing."

~ Micheline (Mitch) Dulude, Veteran

"From the moment I started reading Louise's book I knew I wasn't going to be able to put it down, and I was right. Her story kept me captivated from beginning to end. I would recommend this book to anyone who is interested in how spiritual gifts impact your life."

~ Jayne Lowell, 7-Figure Mindset Mentor

"*Seven Roses* is an incredible story. The book is wonderfully written and will grip you from the emotional beginning through the intrigue at the end. The tumultuous life that this main character, Ellen, has led is mind blowing."

~ Judy O'Beirn, International Bestselling Author of *Unwavering Strength* book series

L.L. TREMBLAY

SEVEN ROSES
INSPIRED BY REAL EVENTS

Hasmark
PUBLISHING
INTERNATIONAL

Editor: Michelle Sugar
msugar@uwo.ca

Proofreader: Corinne Casazza
corinnecasazza@gmail.com

Cover and Book Layout: Anne Karklins
anne@hasmarkpublishing.com

Cover photo: Tongsai/Shutterstock.com

To my amazing son Patrick,
and all my angels,
I love you to the moon and back.

PREFACE

When I was seven years old, I lost myself—day or night, eyes opened or closed, it made no difference. My dreams, nightmares, and realities began to merge into one as they travelled through a maze of confusion and mystical encounters. Words and images continually danced in my head, as if they were doing an aggressive tango. I felt alone amongst those who only believed in tangible realities and could easily rationalize their encounters with the inexplicable. As I began to connect the dots between people, events, and dates, it became apparent that the number seven pervaded every aspect of my life.

No one knows what the future holds –
unless the future warns you.

CHAPTER ONE
TRAGEDY

Sunday, September 17, 1967

I woke up to the sun shining through a small crack in the closed curtains. I stretched my arms and hit my sister Beth's forehead in the process, and she woke up abruptly and started to cry. "Are you okay, Beth? I'm sorry, it was an accident," I claimed, as I kissed her cheek. "Go back to sleep, it's still early," I added, as I pulled the blanket over her small body. I got out of bed, put on my favourite yellow dress, and went to sit at the kitchen table to eat my toast and drink my milk. In a hurry to leave, I dragged my chair back from the table as I got up. It scratched the floor, which was already covered in scars from years of endless abuse. The shrill noise reminded me of my mother and her immeasurable aggravation whenever she heard this noise. "How many times do I need to say this, Ellen—do not drag your chair on the floor! Is that really so difficult?" I usually didn't reply, being anxious to escape her angry look.

"And just where do you think you're going, missy?"

"To Anna's house."

"Well then, take your little brother with you."

"No! Please, Mommy, he's a handful. I don't want to watch him the entire time."

To my surprise, she didn't insist.

"Just make sure you're back for lunch," she said in a seemingly commending tone.

I left and accidentally slammed the door behind me. I turned back and saw my mother peeking through the curtains of our living room window. I waved at her, hoping she wasn't mad at me for slamming it. I worried that it would be considered bad in the eyes of God. My mother warned me about that all the time. She'd say, "If you do something bad, God will punish you." Those words instilled a fear far greater than anything I had ever felt.

• • •

Two hours later, I rubbed the crimson blood that soaked my hands onto my dress as my body violently shook. The word punishment flashed before my eyes. My tears streaked the blood that covered my face, rolling down like hot lava on the side of a volcano. I tried to scream, but I couldn't—a massive lump in my throat blocked the sound, and I was condemned to silence.

"What's your name?" asked the man as he leaned over me.

I struggled not to throw up.

"Ellen. Ellen Taylor."

"How old are you, Ellen?"

"Seven."

He extended his right hand to help me up.

"Are you okay?"

How could I possibly be okay?

I shook my head and began to run as fast as my legs could carry me.

• • •

My family and I lived in a small town in northern Canada that had a population of barely five thousand. Like many families in our neighbourhood, we lived on the edge of poverty. Our white stucco home stood modestly on the side of a busy street. The wraparound porch was by far its best feature because it offered a perfect lookout point for me to watch the people and cars rush by. We lived on the main floor of a two-story house. The house's interior, which was just short of eight hundred square feet, was tight for a family of seven. My two brothers, James and Daniel, slept in bunk beds in one of the three bedrooms, and I shared a bedroom with my sisters, Catherine and Beth.

My father had to work two jobs to make ends meet. He was a salesman by day and a musician by night. He had a good heart, but alcohol was his enemy, and he frequently had a pint too many when he played with his band. I have vivid memories of him coming home during the wee hours of the night, and, charged with a bag of stinging insults, he regularly unloaded them onto my mother like a swarm of wasps. But, rather than fighting back, she would just sit at the kitchen table and smoke her Players cigarette as she did everything she could to conceal her tears.

My bedroom was situated next to the kitchen, so I could hear everything. Even when I tried placing a pillow over my head to block his tirades out, his cruel words cut through me like a million sharp knives. The next morning, I would go to school as if nothing happened, forever burying the secret about what went on within the confines of my house. My mother always reminded me that, "What happens at home is no one else's business," and, as much as it hurt me, I stayed silent.

· · ·

My best friend, Anna, was my solace and escape. She looked like a princess, and that's exactly what her parents called her. She always wore pretty dresses that matched her sparkly green eyes. Everyone was envious of her beautiful long hair, which glistened as it twisted around in its golden spirals. I wish I had hair like hers, my dark brown, mid-length straight hair didn't compare. My mother said that the color of my hair looked better with my hazel eyes, but I still envied everything about Anna, even though I was told that envy was a sin. I didn't know what the word *sin* meant, but it didn't sound good to me.

That year, we were starting our first grade of school. Out of all the new students, I was the only one who didn't wear a uniform because my father couldn't afford to buy me one. Instead, I was forced to wear my black and white polka dot dress—it made me stand out like a sore thumb, and all the kids picked on me. No matter how hard I tried, I just didn't fit in.

A week after school started, my teacher pulled me aside and sent me to the principal's office. "This can't be good," I thought to myself, as I turned the corner of the long corridor and saw Sister Claire leaning against the doorframe of her office. She looked so official in her black nun's attire. She reminded me of my grandmother, with the creases on her face that looked like a map of the world and, even though she wore a veil, I could see the white ray of her hair as it contoured the edge of her forehead. She looked old, but her traits were soft. She waved me in.

"Did I do something wrong?" I asked, as my eyes scanned the large silver cross that was dangling from her neck.

"I have a surprise for you, dear."

She pulled out a large paper bag from the closet next to her desk.

"Open it," she urged.

I took my time, scared that something might jump out at me.

"Go on, dear. It won't bite you!" she said, in a soft but authoritative voice.

I teared up when I saw the dark blue tunic and white blouse, neatly folded in the bag. She reached for a handkerchief in her pocket and wiped the corners of my eyes with it.

"Good heavens. I hope those are happy tears!" she winked.

•   •   •

Sunday, September 17, 1967

Anna lived a few houses down from me, and I ran as quickly as I could to get there. My fluffy yellow dress bounced around like the crinoline of a ballet dancer's tutu. Perhaps this was one of the last times I could wear it before the coolness of autumn settled in. Dolores, the lady who lived above my house, bought it for me. I always liked her—she looked like a porcelain doll with her jet-black hair, blue eyes, and flawless skin. "When I have kids, I hope to have a little girl just like you, Ellen," she'd say. Her words warmed my heart.

I rang the doorbell, and Anna's mother answered. She was dressed like she was going to church, with her respectable cream blouse and turquoise skirt. She had her blonde hair neatly tied back in a bun and she smelled just like fresh flowers. "Come in, Ellen. Anna should be down in a minute, she's just brushing her teeth."

The house looked spotless and beautifully decorated, like those featured in the glossy pages of a home decor magazine. Anna's bedroom was every little girl's dream. It looked like a Barbie house with its canopy bed and laced wallpaper. Standing in the hallway of the entrance, I noticed some black and white family photos on a small wooden table, including a picture of Anna and me that was displayed in a pink photo frame. I secretly wished that I had a picture of her in my own house. The sound of Anna's footsteps as she ran down the hallway startled me for a moment, until she appeared, wearing a dress that resembled mine. Anna and I were like sisters, and even though we were around the same height, we didn't look anything alike except for the freckles on our noses and cheeks.

"Hi, Ellen!" she said, taking my hand and leading me down the hallway.

Like always, we gave each other a hug, and then she put on her shoes and grabbed her rubber ball from the entrance closet.

"Don't go too far, Anna," said her mother.

"Can Ellen eat lunch with us today, Mommy?"

"Sure, if her mother is okay with it."

"I love you, Mommy."

"I love you too, sweetheart."

They blew kisses at each other, and then we stepped out through the door. We made it to the park, just a block away. When we got there, we bounced the ball back and forth across the pavement. It went sideways and rolled across the road, so Anna ran after it and I stayed behind—I wasn't allowed to cross the street, my mother made that very clear. If I did, I'd be punished.

Anna picked up the ball and stood on the curb, waiting for the traffic to clear. An oncoming truck came to a halt, as its driver stuck his hand out the window and signaled for her to cross. When she didn't move, he signaled her again, more assiduously this time. I waved at her from across the street. "Come on, Anna!" I shouted. Seemingly out of nowhere, a white van began to quickly pass the truck as it sat motionless on the road. I screamed at the top of my lungs, "Anna! Stop! STOP!"

I watched in pure horror as the van hit her. Her tiny body went flying in midair, like it was moving in slow motion, until it came crashing to the ground like a brick. I screamed so loud that the whole neighbourhood seemed to shake, and then leapt to the middle of the street and fell on my knees, next to Anna's body, which was completely covered in blood. Sitting motionless and in shock, I couldn't even begin to comprehend what I had just witnessed.

"Wake up, Anna. Anna, wake up!" I clamoured.

I saw the driver of the van shriek as he repeatedly banged his head on the steering wheel, like he was trying to wake himself up from this nightmare. Then, the driver of the truck bolted out of his vehicle and ran to Anna's side. "No, no, no, no! God, please no," he lamented. My body trembled like it was 40-degrees below zero. "Please God, let this be a bad dream," I silently pleaded, hoping that somewhere he was listening. Soon, the street became crowded with helpless bystanders and then, as I held Anna's hand over my heart, I heard a hysterical scream. I turned my head and saw Anna's mother run towards me in a panic. She threw herself over her daughter's body and howled desperately, "Oh God, please don't take my baby, she's only seven!"

I felt helpless and scared, and as I cried, a butterfly with bright pink wings landed on my shoulder. In that moment, I felt a sense of calm wash over me. I leaned down and kissed Anna on her cheek and whispered, "I love you to the moon and back, Anna." I heard her mother say that to her once. Anna's mother looked at me with disgust as she snatched my arm and aggressively shook it, the butterfly remaining on my shoulder.

"Ellen, *what* happened?"

I shivered in fear, and then I told her. She slapped my face with the back of her hand. "This is all your fault, Ellen!" she shouted.

Her words stabbed me in the heart, and I felt guilty.

"Get away from her," she said, looking at me with wrath in her eyes.

"Ma'am, please calm down," said the policeman who finally arrived on the scene. "She's just a little girl," he added.

I wobbled over to the sidewalk and sat down—my body cold as ice. Although Anna didn't show any signs of life, the paramedics continued their attempts to revive her.

"Are you okay?" asked the policeman.

I didn't answer. He extended his hand to me to help me up.

I looked at my blood-stained dress and anticipated my mother's impending fury. I began running, my legs so weak that every step I took caused me to experience immense pain. Surprisingly, the butterfly followed me home as it clung to my shoulder. My heart stopped when I saw my mother on the porch, she looked worried and upset at the same time.

"Ellen, are you okay? I heard the sirens—"

"It's Anna, Mommy, she—"

"What happened? Why are you covered in blood?"

When she realized that I was in shock and couldn't talk, she took Beth inside and put her in her crib. I sat on the porch, shaking uncontrollably. Daniel—my four-year-old brother—sat beside me.

"Why are you bleeding, Ellen?"

My mother came back outside before I could say anything.

"Daniel, go back in the house and check on Beth."

"Ellen, you need to tell me what happened right now," she insisted, as Daniel hesitantly moved inside.

I needed a hug more than anything.

"Anna was hit by a car—I watched her die, Mommy!" pouring my heart out.

"Oh my God, Ellen! You were with her? How did it happen?"

"She ran across the street to get a ball we were playing with and—"

"She crossed the busy street? Why didn't you stop her?"

This was all my fault—I knew it. She pulled me into the bathroom and washed the blood off my face and hands.

"This is what happens when you don't listen, Ellen."

"What did I do wrong, Mommy?"

"You know exactly what you did wrong, young lady!"

No, not really.

"Look at you, your dress is ruined now."

"I'm sorry, Mommy."

"Put your pajamas on and go to bed, you need to rest."

What I needed was for my mother to comfort me.

I heard her talk to my father on the phone. "What if she had crossed the street too, John? She could have been killed!" she said, her voice crackling.

It should have been me, I thought.

CHAPTER TWO

FAREWELL

I was on the edge of sleep when I heard someone whisper my name. My body rested motionless on what felt like a bed of sand, I was sinking and couldn't move a muscle. The lights flickered on and off as I let out a faint scream and saw my mother standing at the entrance.

"Ellen, is everything okay?"

I couldn't speak.

"I heard you screaming. What's wrong?"

I stared at her in silence as she moved slowly beside me and placed her hand on my forehead, looking concerned.

"I think you have a fever. I'll get you some aspirin."

I grabbed her hand. I didn't want her to leave me, it was too scary to be alone.

"I'll be right back," she said.

She came back five minutes later with two baby aspirins and a glass of water.

"Take this. I called the doctor, he's coming over after dinner."

My body trembled uncontrollably.

"I'll make some chicken soup, it'll make you feel better," she said.

How can chicken soup make me feel better?

She left and turned off the lights on her way out.

"Mommy, please leave the lights on!" I screamed. She flipped the switch up and down, but the room remained in complete darkness.

"The light bulb must have burned out. I'll ask your father to change it when he gets home."

I hated being left alone in the dark. I pulled the blanket over my head, convinced that it would offer me some sort of protection. As I drifted off, an eerie feeling, almost like someone was watching me, jolted me awake. I pulled the blanket off my head and opened my eyes, and I saw a white shadow standing at the foot of my bed. At first, I thought that it might be one of my sisters, but after I rubbed my eyes it became clearer—it was a little girl and she was smiling at me. She whispered, "Ellen, it's me. Anna." I bolted upright in a cold sweat, my heart racing.

"Anna?"

"Yes, Ellen."

"But you're supposed to be dead—"

"I am dead."

"Does that mean… wait, am I dead too?"

"No, silly. I just came back to tell you that what happened today is not your fault."

I panicked and let out a piercing scream, which prompted my mother to come running into the bedroom.

"Ellen, what's going on?"

"It's Anna. She's here, Mommy!" pointing to where my best friend had just stood seconds ago.

"What are you talking about? Anna is dead, Ellen. You had a bad dream, that's all."

No, it wasn't a dream.

She put her right hand on my forehead again to see if my fever had gone down.

"You're still quite warm, but don't worry, the doctor should be here anytime now."

As she left, I pulled the blanket over my head again, needing protection now more than ever. My mother came back a few minutes later with an onion she had cut in half, placing one half under each of my feet and then covering them with socks. This was an old medicine trick that my grandmother passed down to us—apparently, onions absorbed a fever.

The doctor arrived ten minutes later. He reminded me of Santa Claus, with his white hair and long white beard. After examining me, he said that my fever was likely a symptom of my trauma from earlier that day.

"She needs to rest. Give her two aspirins every four hours and call me in the morning if her condition doesn't improve."

"You heard the doctor, Ellen. Go to sleep, and you'll feel better in the morning."

When my father got home from work, he came to see me. I woke up when he placed his cold hand on my left cheek.

"How are you feeling, Ellen?"

I could smell cigarettes on his hands—I hated that smell.

"Your mother told me what happened today," he said, rubbing my shoulder.

"Did she tell you that Anna was in my room earlier?" I answered.

"She did. You had a dream, Ellen. That's all it was."

"It wasn't a dream, Daddy. I saw her. She talked to me!" I yelled, getting worked up.

"Listen to me, Ellen. Ghosts don't exist, trust me," he insisted.

They do.

"Can you change the light bulb, Daddy?"

"What's wrong with it?"

He turned on the switch, and then light flooded the room.

"Hmm, it seems fine," he said, looking confused. "Your mother made some chicken soup if you're hungry."

"I'm not hungry," I answered bluntly, pulling the blanket back over my head.

• • •

The next morning, I woke up to the smell of bacon and eggs. I dragged myself out of bed and went to the kitchen.

"You must be hungry, Ellen. You didn't eat anything yesterday," my mother said as I sat down at the table.

I stared at the plate of food in front of me—I had no appetite.

"Mommy, what's going to happen to Anna now?" I asked delicately, unsure if I really wanted to know.

"Well, there will be a wake, and then a mass before the burial ceremony."

I didn't understand a word of that.

"What is a *wake*?" I asked.

"Her body will be placed in an open casket for people to pay their last respects," she answered.

I still didn't understand.

"And the *burial*, what is that?"

"That is when they lower the casket into the ground."

"Into the ground? But she won't be able to breathe—"

"Ellen, Anna is dead. She doesn't need to breathe anymore."

How could she say that?

"But I saw her in my room last night," I insisted, hoping that this would convince her. "She's not dead! She talked to me –"

"Ellen, stop that nonsense right now!" my mother interrupted. "People will think you're crazy, for God's sake."

"I'm not crazy," I said, sobbing.

"Eat your breakfast and stop crying, you'll upset your little sister," she said coldly, pushing the unappetizing plate of breakfast closer to me.

• • •

On the day of the funeral, my mother asked if I still wanted to go. I said yes—I didn't think I had a choice.

"What do I wear, Mommy?"

"You don't have anything that's all black, so I suppose you'll just have to wear your polka dot dress."

I hated that dress, it was getting too small for me.

She tried to lighten the dark circles under my eyes with makeup. I looked like someone had punched me in the face. My sister,

Catherine, brushed my hair and pulled it back into a ponytail. "It's going to be okay, Ellen," she said, as she rubbed my back. She wanted to come too, but she had to stay home with my brothers and sister. She was like a mother to me, to all of us. I looked up to her, and I wanted to be just like her one day. She had dyed her hair jet black and always had it up in a beehive. She wore makeup and fake eyelashes, which made her already gorgeous green eyes stand out even more.

My mother wore her black dress, which looked a little too tight on her, and she put on a pair of black high heels. This was one of the rare occasions I saw her all dressed up, she looked beautiful. Her flawless skin didn't need makeup, so she simply coated her lips with scarlet red lipstick and applied a thin layer of black mascara on her eyelashes. The black fishnet headpiece that she attached to her carefully styled hair made her look taller, at least a couple of notches above her five-foot-two inch frame.

The funeral home was in walking distance from our house, and just a few steps away from the church. When we arrived, a tall skinny man dressed in black opened the door for us. His scruffy grey hair and bushy eyebrows made him look old and sad, like he had encountered too many dead people in his life. I wanted to run away, but my mother pulled me in.

A shiver ran down my spine when I saw the white casket raised on a red velvet pedestal, surrounded by dozens of colourful flowers. I noticed Anna's mother and father standing in front of it. Will she be mad to see me there? I wondered. My mother tugged on my arm to prompt me to walk forward, and when I tried to grip her hand she shook it lose. We walked slowly towards the casket, my knees weakened—I felt sick. The overwhelming aroma of burnt incense mixed with the musty wood smell of the gloomy building turned my stomach. It reminded me of my grandparent's home.

"Mommy, I think I'm going to be sick."

"It's just nerves, Ellen. Take a deep breath, you'll be fine."

But the smell.

My mother helped me as I tried to climb up onto the step where

Anna's body rested. I stood on the tip of my toes to look at her, my hands gripping the edge of the casket. She looked like a wax doll, and nothing at all like the beautiful girl I had known just a couple of days before. She was holding a pink rose in her hands. "Why did they cut her hair, Mommy?" I asked hesitantly. "Shhh! Be quiet, Ellen," she hissed. I took another look before I stepped down, refusing to believe that it was Anna in that box. I tugged on my mother's dress. "Can we go now?"

"Not yet, we have to wait until they take the casket to the church," she whispered, barely moving her red lips.

Although Anna's mother was just a couple of inches away, she refused to make eye contact with either of us. Her husband glanced over, bowing his head in a somber salute. Finally, they closed the casket, and four men in black carried it to a hearse that was parked in front of the funeral home. They drove it to the church, while everyone else followed on foot.

The church filled up with family, friends, and a surprising number of strangers who had been touched by the tragedy. The loud sound of the pipe organ penetrated my body right through to my soul. It made me cry. I think that's the purpose of playing music like that—to make everyone upset. The priest stood in front of the pedestal, and we could barely hear him speak, amid all the sniffing and sobbing.

"We are gathered here today to say farewell to Anna and to commit her into the hands of God," he declared.

Why did God have to take her?

He went on to say that life was precious and could be taken away from us when we least expected it. His sermon lasted forty-five minutes, but it felt like an eternity.

Anna's father stood up and slowly moved to the front of the church to read his eulogy. He looked so broken, his face covered in tears and his voice trembling. "Anna, my princess, you came into our lives like a breath of fresh air. You brought us joy and happiness when we needed it most. At only seven years old, your life had just begun. You didn't deserve to die, especially not in that way. We will never understand God's decision to take you from us, but we trust that he needs you more than we do.

We miss you more than words can say, and we can't wait to see you again in heaven, where we will be reunited for eternity.

Rest in peace, my sweet love."

After he concluded this heartfelt speech to his daughter, I looked over and saw that even my mother was crying. Anna's mother was inconsolable, and I sat motionless, praying that this was just a bad dream. The pastor made the sign of the cross over the casket and recited, "Lord, you gave her life, now receive her in your peace and give her, through Jesus Christ, a joyful resurrection."

Resurrection?

As we exited the church, I let go of my mother's hand, and I hastily ran to the side of the building and hid behind a tree and threw up. My mother came looking for me. "Oh, Ellen, look at you, you made a mess of your dress." She took a handkerchief from her black purse and wiped my mouth and my dress with it. "Hang in there, it's almost over," she said, looking somewhat distressed with her hair disheveled and her mascara in streaks down her face.

The cemetery wasn't far from the church, but it felt like such a long walk. Our neighbour, Mr. Clark, offered us a ride. My mother and I sat in the back of his white station wagon, while Corinne, Mr. Clark's wife, took a couple of cigarettes out of a silver metal case. She gave one to my mother. I grimaced and covered my nose with the side of my dress. "Are you okay, Ellen?" asked Mr. Clark, lighting the end of her cigarette. My mother snapped, "Don't worry about it, she's just being fussy, as usual."

When we arrived at the cemetery, the frigid air made my legs feel weak and shaky. We weaved around a sea of towering tombstones to get to Anna's grave, and, when we got closer, I saw Anna's mother howling in grief and spreading her arms wide over the casket, unwilling to let it go. As they began to lower it into the ground, I started to wonder if my mother would be as devastated if I died.

The fact that I envied Anna even now troubled me.

After the casket was lowered down, people lined up to place a flower on top of it. When my turn came, I kneeled and gently put down a pink rose, tears cascading down my face. "Goodbye, Anna," I whispered, blowing kisses to her. A butterfly fluttered to my shoulder, making me feel instantly calm.

At the end of the ceremony, Mr. Clark drove us home, and I went to bed right away. Not long after I had drifted off, I was woken up by a strange dream that felt very real. I imagined myself flying like a bird through a white tunnel, and at the end of it I saw seven people sitting at a rectangular table. Everything was white— the walls, the table, the chairs, the floor, their clothes—except for one little girl in a light pink dress. She looked at me and smiled. I woke up abruptly to the voice of my mother calling me to the kitchen for dinner. I wasn't hungry, I just wanted to go back to my dream and stay with Anna, and pretend that the accident never happened.

I wish I never had to find out about the sadness of death and burials. It was more than my young, innocent mind could take.

CHAPTER THREE
A NEW FRIEND

After Anna's funeral, I locked myself inside my bedroom, buried under a dark cloud that descended over my thoughts and emotions. I had no motivation or energy for anything—I could barely get out of bed, let alone eat—and all I wanted to do was shut out the world. As I drifted in and out of sleep, I heard my mother speaking sternly to my doctor on the phone. "No, there's no way I am giving her medication for depression. She's only seven for God's sake! I'll just keep her at home for the next few days. It will pass." When she came in to check on me, I asked my mother what 'depression' meant. "It's when someone feels sad and hopeless all the time," she said in a casual and dismissive tone. "But don't you worry about that, Ellen, you're way too young to be depressed," she insisted, tightly shutting the door as she left my room.

I started to feel a bit better as the week progressed. When I finally got out of bed the following Sunday, I put on some clean clothes and ate a small breakfast, which prompted my mother to revel in the accuracy of her diagnosis. "See? I knew there was nothing to worry about! How could you be depressed? Now you can make yourself useful around here and finally go back to school tomorrow." I didn't want to, but I knew that I had no say in this matter.

The next day, my sister Catherine walked with me to school, and as we passed by the scene of the accident, I started to cry. "It's my fault, you know," I stuttered, remembering the horrible events that took place there. Catherine immediately tried to comfort me, putting her arm around my shoulders, "This wasn't your fault, Ellen. It was an accident," she answered, trying to make me feel better. No matter what anyone said, though, I still felt guilty. When we reached my school, she stayed with me until the bell rang and then promised that she'd be back to get me later. As I climbed the stairs up to the wooden front doors of the building, I found myself wondering whether I was supposed to act like this life-changing event never occurred. I felt that dark cloud creeping back, but I tried to push it away as I went inside.

When I entered the classroom, my heart sank when I saw Anna's pencil and notebook lying on her desk waiting for her. The teacher called out each student's name one by one, noting their presence. When she accidentally called Anna's name, I swear I heard her say, "Present!" The teacher quickly apologized for her mistake, scratching my best friend's name from her list. For the rest of the day, I found it very difficult to concentrate, all I could do was stare at Anna's empty desk and wish that she was sitting there smiling back at me.

When the bell rang at four o'clock, I bolted out of my chair and ran to meet Catherine, but she was nowhere to be found. After fifteen minutes, I decided to walk back alone, and when I got home, I asked my mother why Catherine didn't meet me. She said that she was called into work and that it didn't matter because I was old enough to walk home by myself.

She had no idea how wrong she was.

That night, I had another strange dream. I was in a house I'd never seen before, and was greeted by a seven-year-old boy who took me by the hand and led me down a long and narrow corridor, which was lined with seven closed doors. Their white paint was flaking, revealing previous coats of blues and grey, and each of them had a brass doorknob with a butterfly carved onto it.

The house's old hardwood floors squeaked as we went down the hallway, and even though I didn't know where I was, I felt safe with the boy. As we proceeded down the hallway, he opened each door one by one. The seventh door, however, was locked and wouldn't budge, no matter how much he tried to force the knob to turn. It was this loud rattling that jolted me out of sleep, and as soon as I woke up, I ran into the kitchen to tell my mother about the peculiar dreams I was having lately. "Your mind is playing tricks on you, Ellen. Just remember, dreams aren't real!" she ardently insisted. They sure felt real to me, but I didn't insist.

• • •

One month after the accident, I made a new friend. Vicki was the same age as me and she lived on the street behind ours. I had seen her before because our backyards were adjacent, but I had never made the effort to speak to her. I liked Vicki, she looked like an Amazonian princess with her beautiful black hair, chocolate brown round eyes, and tanned complexion. Although I knew that she would never replace Anna, I was happy to have a new friend to walk to school with and someone to talk to.

Since Halloween was coming up, Vicki asked me to go trick-or-treating with her, and I immediately said yes—I loved Halloween! When the night finally arrived, we put on our ghost costumes, just simple white linen bedsheets with scissor-cut eyeholes, and headed out the door to join the other children, who were also disguised as ghosts. Everyone held glowing yellow lanterns that looked mesmerizing as they walked down the streets. I wondered if Anna might be hiding amid all the ghosts walking the streets— I felt her presence. After going door-to-door and visiting as many houses as we possibly could, we returned home with our pillow cases filled with apples, molasses candies, and other treats. This was the first night in a long time that I experienced some semblance of joy, and I found myself thinking that maybe everything would be okay.

• • •

Fall swiftly came and went, and before I knew it the first snow-fall of the season swept in. "Ellen, wake up, wake up!" yelled my little brother. "What is it, Daniel?"

"Look, it's snowing!" he said, jumping up and down on my bed and pulling the bedroom curtains open to reveal the thick, white carpet of snow in the backyard. "Ellen, can you play outside in the snow with me?" he asked. I didn't feel like it, but my mother answered for me. "Yes, of course she'll go with you, Daniel." Then she turned to me and said, "It'll do you some good, Ellen. You need to take your mind off things." Conceding like always, I obeyed her and changed my clothes and then followed my brother outside.

"Ellen, can you help me make a snowman?" Daniel asked, his big blue eyes sparkling with hope as we made snow angels. The snow didn't stick too well but we still managed to build a figure that resembled a snowman. Daniel looked frozen, his cheeks had turned as red as a candy apple. "Time to go in before your face cracks!" I said, pointing to the back door of our house. I decided to stay outside for a couple of minutes more, sitting down on the soft snow to inspect our creation. Then, I noticed a dark and peculiar spot on the snowman's face, so I got up to see what it was. As I got closer and touched his face, I realised that there was blood dripping down from his buttoned eyes, and I immediately ran into the house.

"What's wrong, Ellen?" my mother asked, sitting at the kitchen table reading the newspaper. I showed her my finger.

"How'd you do that?" she asked.

"Do what?"

"Cut your finger!" she responded, looking confused.

"I didn't cut my finger! The snowman was crying tears of blood!" I shrieked, praying that she'd finally believe me.

"Dear God, here we go again!" she said, dismissing my distress. She got up and started making hot chocolate while Daniel and I sat at the table with our colouring books and crayons.

"Ellen, what do ghosts look like?" Daniel asked, out of nowhere.

"What are you talking about?"

"I heard you talk about ghosts with Mommy the other day."

"It's complicated, Daniel. We can't always see them, and sometimes they look like people." I answered, trying to be as vague as I could. This kind of thing is too scary for someone so young, I thought.

"They look like regular people?"

"Yeah, like my friend Anna, for example."

"Anna is dead, Ellen."

"Yes, but that's what ghosts are—they're dead."

"I'm scared, Ellen. Will the ghosts come and hurt me?" he asked, tears welling up in his eyes.

"No, Daniel, you don't need to worry, I promise."

My mother was silently listening to every word of our conversation—I almost forgot that she was in the room with us. Her patience wore out and she turned towards us, her face beat red with anger. "Ellen, if I hear you talk about ghosts one more time, you'll be grounded for a month! Do you hear me? This has gone too far!" she hissed, slapping my arm with the back of her hand.

"But I wasn't talking about it! Daniel just asked me a question—"

"Go to your room! Now!" she interjected, completely unwilling to listen to me.

In my room, as I collected my thoughts, I began to wonder if it was Anna who made the snowman cry tears of blood. Maybe it was her way of letting me know she missed playing with me.

CHAPTER FOUR

AFTERMATH

Just a couple of weeks later, an old lady was struck and killed by a car at the same intersection where Anna died. The neighbourhood was outraged. People rallied to put pressure on the city to install traffic lights—Anna's parents led the movement—and eventually they agreed to put up the lights in the spring.

I became very curious about this lady, and on the day of her funeral, I decided to sneak away by myself to the church. I didn't know her, but something urged me to go. I sat in the back of the church and flipped through a small book of photos and memorable stories from her life. After the short mass, everyone left, brushing past me as if I were invisible. I found that strange—not even the priest looked at me. I went home and didn't mention any of this to my mother because she'd probably call me morbid and send me to my room again.

That night, I dreamt about the old lady. Her white and short and curly hair dangled out from under her magenta hat. I could tell she was a nice person just by her friendly eyes and welcoming smile. She was dressed exactly like she was in one of the pictures I saw of her at the church. She wore a grey angora shawl over her shoulders, along with a bright, lilac coloured dress. She appeared with light around her body and she smiled at me, just like an angel. I had no idea why or how, but I felt connected to her.

. . .

On Christmas Eve, my father went to a nearby store to purchase a tree and some gifts—he always did things last minute so that he could buy everything on sale. Catherine had a sleepover at her friend's house that night, and she told me that I could sleep in her bed, which was a real treat because Beth wet our bed every night. We went to sleep early in anticipation of opening our gifts first thing the next morning. I had just put my head on the pillow when I felt fingers stroking my hair. I jumped upright, hitting my head on the headboard in the process, and I saw Anna in her pink dress, sitting gracefully on the edge of my bed.

"Anna! What are you doing here?"

"I need to talk to you," she said, looking exactly the same as she had before the accident.

Beth woke up and saw me sitting upright, talking to someone in the dark.

"Ellen, who are you talking to?" she asked, with a hint of fear in her voice.

"Nobody. Go back to sleep, Beth!"

By the time I looked back to where Anna was sitting, she was gone. I kept my eyes wide open for the rest of the night, hoping she would come back.

The next morning, Beth didn't wait a second to tell my mother about what had happened the night before. "Mommy, Ellen was talking to a ghost last night," she said matter-of-factly, unwilling to keep quiet even when I put my hand over her mouth. She was only three years old, but boy could she ever talk!

"What are you talking about, Beth?" asked my mother.

"I heard her talking to someone last night while I was trying to sleep."

"She just had a bad dream, Beth, don't worry about it."

My mother grabbed me by the arm and pulled me into the living room.

"Ellen, you have to stop this nonsense once and for all! Your brother isn't enough? Now you're trying to scare your little sister?"

"But Anna was in my room and she—"

"Stop it! If you keep this up, I'll take you to the doctor and he'll give you a needle," she threatened, knowing that I would concede because I was so afraid of them.

"But why won't you believe me, Mommy?"

"Because Anna is dead, and ghosts don't exist. Get it? Quit your sobbing, it's Christmas! Can't we just have one normal day?" I decided to let her win this one, and we went back into the kitchen and ate in silence.

After breakfast, we gathered around the Christmas tree to open our gifts. My father handed me a box that was wrapped in brown paper and embellished with colourful stars. "This is from Santa Claus," he winked. I excitedly ripped the paper and was thrilled to unveil the Skipper Barbie Doll I had wanted for so long. Anna had at least four Barbie Dolls, and we use to play with them all the time. Skipper was beautiful, with long blonde hair that covered the front of her bright red bathing suit. Beth got a pink teddy bear, and Daniel a red fire truck toy, while Catherine and James didn't get anything—my parents said that they were too old, but I knew the real reason was that my father couldn't afford it.

• • •

As time went on, I saw Anna more and more. While I never really got used to it, her appearances didn't surprise me as much as they had before. The hardest part about all of this was that I couldn't tell anyone about seeing her or about my recurring dreams of the hallway with the seven doors and the white tunnel. I became obsessed with trying to connect the dots. What was behind the seventh door and why was it locked? Why did I always wake up before the boy could open it? Why did more and more people start to appear in the white tunnel? These questions drove me out of my mind. Having the same dreams over and over also made me question whether my real life was a dream, or if my dreams were my real life. Nothing made sense anymore.

. . .

That weekend, I made clothes for my Barbie Doll out of an old flowery smock my mother had given me. I cut it into square pieces and made two dresses, a long one and a short one. They weren't perfect, but I was proud of them. I put the short dress on Skipper and tied her hair in a ponytail. She reminded me of Anna—I still didn't understand why her long curls were cut when I saw her at the wake, and no matter how hard I tried I couldn't get this image out of my mind.

"Mommy, why did they cut Anna's hair when she died?" I asked as I entered the kitchen and found my mother washing dishes.

"I don't know, Ellen, I guess because her mother wanted to keep it."

"Do you think she would give me a piece of it?"

"It's called a 'lock', Ellen. But I suppose you could always ask her and see what she says."

Without any hesitation, I put on my jacket and boots and ran over to Anna's house. Standing on her front steps, I noticed that the doorbell had been removed. I took a deep breath before I knocked. Anna's mother opened the door halfway, and I was surprised to see her in a nightgown in the middle of the afternoon. She looked nothing like the woman who hugged Anna goodbye before we went to play with the bouncy ball just a few months before. She had cut her hair short and dyed it black and, instead of smelling like sweet flowers, she reeked of cigarette smoke.

"What are you doing here? What do you want?"

"Um… hi, Mrs. Evans. Would it be possible to have a lock of Anna's hair please?" I delicately inquired, praying that she wouldn't start screaming at me.

"What makes you think I kept her hair?"

She didn't wait for a reply. "You have some nerve coming here and asking me for anything, Ellen Taylor, especially something that's so personal! Anna would still be here if it weren't for you. I don't want you to come here ever again. Do you understand me?"

I had never seen her this mad before, but her eyes revealed that her rage really came from her immense despair and longing for her daughter. Her husband heard our exchange and came to the door.

"Hi, Ellen. Nicole, what's going on here?" he asked, looking confused and somewhat alarmed. She looked at him and stayed silent, then slammed the door in my face. It crushed me, and I ran back home in tears. My mother was on the porch smoking a cigarette and looked concerned as I approached her empty-handed. "Let me guess, she didn't give it to you?" I started to cry. "Just forget about it," she said, as she threw her cigarette butt onto the front lawn.

If only it were that easy.

• • •

Before I knew it, it was Easter Sunday, and Vicki invited me to her house for an Easter egg hunt. I was excited because we never did anything like this at home. I rode my rusty bicycle to her place—though I was getting too big for it, but I didn't care. When I arrived, Vicki's mother opened the door, "Come in, Ellen. Are you ready for some fun?" Earlier that day, Vicki's mother had hidden plastic eggs around the backyard. We had a blast hunting for them, but we mostly enjoyed eating the chocolate and candies hidden inside. We ate so much our stomachs hurt, and then we spent the rest of the afternoon rocking in the hammock her father had hitched between two enormous trees. It felt good to do something normal and fun with a friend, and it made me forget about all the strange things that kept happening lately—at least temporarily.

• • •

When the end of the school year finally came, I graduated first grade with flying colours. My teacher gave me a gift that was wrapped in flower print paper—I loved it so much that I didn't want to rip it. "Go on, Ellen, open it," she said. My face lit up when I saw a beautiful hardcover book with the words *Alice's Adventures in Wonderland* written across the top. It occurred to me that this was the first book I ever owned, and it made me smile so much that my cheeks hurt. I hugged my teacher and thanked her for the gift, and as I walked down the crowded hall to leave, I felt both happiness and sadness. I tried to bottle my memories of Anna on our first day in that classroom, and how happy I felt when she looked over and made a silly face at me from her desk. I walked out of the school with a heavy heart, but I was happy to see Vicki waiting for me in the schoolyard. She carried a backpack so heavy that she had to lean forward to avoid falling backwards. I had less books than her, which was lucky for me because I didn't have a bag to carry them in. We giggled as we walked home arm-in-arm. When we were almost there, we saw a car parked on the right side of the road with its engine still running, and the driver waved us over as he rolled down the passenger window.

"Girls, where are you going? Want a ride home?"

"No, thank you," I replied, feeling nervous.

"Come closer, I want to show you something."

Reluctant but curious, Vicki pulled me towards the car and together we glanced through the passenger window.

"Look what I have," he said, shaking his 'thing' out of his pants.

We were in shock. I panicked and dropped my books, and Vicki quickly bent down and picked up *Alice's Adventures in Wonderland*, leaving the rest on the ground. I grabbed her hand, and we ran home as fast as we could. When we got closer, she dashed to her house and I went straight to mine, uncontrollably shuddering and feeling nauseous. As soon as I got into the house, I raced to the bathroom and threw up.

"Ellen, are you okay?" asked my mother, standing at the bathroom door.

When I told her what had happened just moments ago, she yelled "What? Oh my gosh! What a pervert!"

I didn't know what pervert was.

"Do you know who this man is?"

"No."

"Have you ever seen him before?"

"No, I don't know who he is, Mommy."

"Listen to me, Ellen, you need to erase what you saw from your memory. He's a sick man!"

I couldn't even comprehend what I saw, but the image was burned into my mind. When my father came home, my mother explained what happened, and he was furious. He sat me down on the couch and then he proceeded to grill me with an endless string of questions.

"What colour was the car? What did the man look like? Was he young or old?"

I had a hard time answering everything because I was too busy looking at what that creepy man was doing and I didn't pay attention to these sorts of details.

"Dark green. His car was dark green!" I exclaimed, happy that I remembered at least something that could help.

"What about his face? Do you remember anything about it?"

"He had dark hair and wore glasses… I think."

My father called Vicki's mother, and she told him that Vicki didn't remember any more details than I did. She said she was going to call the police to report him, and my father did the same. As it turned out, this was not the first time something like this happened. The police officer told my father that they had received several calls in the last few days, but they were unable to find the man. I hardly got any sleep that night—I couldn't stop thinking about that disturbing image I had seen earlier that day.

• • •

During summer vacation, Vicki and I became inseparable. On a sunny Saturday afternoon at the park, she asked what had happened on the day of Anna's accident, but I told her that I didn't want to talk about it because it was too painful.

"Why do you feel guilty, Ellen?" she persisted.

"Because I should've gone to get the ball, not Anna."

"But if you had, then maybe you would be the one who got hit by that car."

"Maybe, but at least Anna would be alive… and her mother wouldn't hate me so much!"

"And Anna would be the one feeling like you are right now."
The words spoken by Vicki didn't sound like they were hers.

I felt something tickle my shoulder, and when I turned my head to see what it was, I saw that same butterfly with pink wings looking back at me.

"This butterfly has been following me around since the day Anna died," I said, pointing to it as it fluttered its wings.

"There are butterflies all over the place, Ellen. It's the summer! There's no way it's the same one."

"It is, I swear! But it's okay if you don't believe me... no one ever does."

I felt a presence around me, and as I turned to look behind me I heard a voice calling my name. At first, I thought it was Vicki, but when I looked over, I noticed that she wasn't there anymore. I scanned the park, thinking she might have gone to sit on the swing or play in the grass, but I couldn't find her. After a while, I decided to go to her house. Maybe she went home without telling me, even though it was unlikely that she'd just leave me there. Her mother answered the door and, when I asked her where Vicki was, she looked at me with a confused expression and said that she was sick that day and had been in bed all morning.

"But she was at the park with me," I said, smiling and thinking that she must be playing a trick on me.

"That's not possible, Ellen. As I said, she hasn't left the house at all today."

It didn't make sense to me, but I thanked her and went home. Was it really Anna at the park the whole time? Nothing was as it seemed, so perhaps it was possible, I thought. I never mentioned anything about it to my mother. What was the point? She wouldn't believe me anyway.

• • •

A year had already passed since Anna died, and no matter how much I tried, my heart wouldn't stop missing her. I sat down on the couch in the living room, where my mother and sister were knitting, and I asked my mother if I could go to the cemetery to visit Anna. "You should wait until tomorrow, Ellen. There's a good chance Anna's parents will be there today. It might be better to avoid them," she said convincingly. I knew Anna's mother didn't want anything to do with me, but silently I hoped that maybe things had changed. "I'll go with you tomorrow, Ellen," Catherine said, feeling sorry for me.

The next day, I got out of bed early and was anxious to leave the house. I put on my purple pants and green shirt and stepped into my worn out running shoes. Like always, my sister needed more time to do her hair and makeup, and she told me to eat something while she finished getting ready. Even though I wasn't hungry, she insisted, so I forced myself to drink a glass of milk that was lukewarm because it was sitting out on the table for too long.

On the way to the cemetery, we stopped at the flower shop. As I gazed at the flowers, Catherine told me to pick one, so I chose a beautiful, perfectly-shaped pink rose. I held it close to my heart all the way to the cemetery. When we got there, I began to feel weak in the knees and my heart was beating faster than usual. I hadn't been to the cemetery since that terrible day a year ago, and the thought of being amongst that many dead people in one place gave me chills. I heard voices all around me. "Can you hear that, Catherine?" I said, my voice shaking. "Hear what?" Catherine answered with a critical look on her face. "Never mind," I answered, as she took my hand and we weaved amongst the tombstones on our way to Anna's. Some of them looked abandoned, swallowed by overgrown weeds. It made me sad. "Here we are," my sister said. Anna's tombstone was in the shape of a cross and the inscription, "Anna Evans 1960–1967" was engraved in ornate letters. At the base of the monument was a large bouquet of fresh flowers, which confirmed that her parents had been there.

I dropped to my knees and cried out, "I miss you so much, Anna." I laid the pink rose on the base of her tombstone and felt a hand on my shoulder. It startled me, and I turned to see who it was, expecting that it was just Catherine trying to console me, but she wasn't there. I jumped when I saw Anna standing directly in front of me. She gazed at me and whispered, "None of this is your fault, Ellen."

I howled Catherine's name, and she came running. "What's wrong, Ellen?"

"Did you see her?"

"Who?"

"Anna! She's right there," I shrieked, pointing to my left. But Anna had disappeared. "Forget it," I said, feeling foolish.

"You must be tired, Ellen. I think it's time for us to go," Catherine said, looking concerned.

She hastily grabbed my hand and we left the cemetery, as I begged her not to say anything to my mother. On our way home, I had a strange feeling that Anna was following us.

"I won't say anything, Ellen, but even you have to admit that you've been acting a little strange lately."

"You don't believe me either, do you?"

"Don't be mad, but I think it's all in your imagination. It will get better as time passes, don't worry about it."

She couldn't be more wrong.

When we got home, my mother had already made lunch and put in on the table—ham sandwiches and pea soup. After I finished eating, I ran outside and hopped on my bicycle to go and see Vicki. Her father opened the door and looked at me funny, which made me feel uncomfortable. "Vicki can't go out today, Ellen," he said, slamming the door in my face. I felt confused and worried about my friend—why did these bizarre things keep happening?

CHAPTER FIVE
MONSTERS DO EXIST

September 1970

By the time I turned ten, I developed a passion for reading—I was obsessed with the power that books had to transport me to another place and time so that I could temporarily escape my own world. Even though I read dozens of books, including *The Adventures of Tintin* series which Vicki loaned me, my favourite was always *Alice's Adventures in Wonderland* because I felt like I could relate to her more than any other character. When Vicki told me that Disney had made an animated movie based on the book, I couldn't wait to see it.

My father bought our first—black and white—television that year, and it pulled our family closer together because we often gathered around it after dinner to watch whatever was playing on any of the three channels available to us. My father's favourite thing to watch was *The Ed Sullivan Show*, and keeping his gaze fixed on the screen, he'd always recall his best memories over the years. "The Beatles performed for the first time on air in 1964," he said, "Ed Sullivan put them on the map." I loved The Beatles! I used to collect all their pictures whenever I got their bubble gum packs—Paul McCartney was my favorite.

The television turned out to be a great distraction for the next few months, but by the time summer arrived, I'd had enough of it and began playing outside more. When the school year ended, I couldn't have been happier. Vicki and I had organized an outdoor pool party in her backyard—I was excited because Vicki's father kept her at home more often, so I hadn't seen much of her except at school. Vicki's mother prepared food platters and made a pitcher of Kool-Aid, and we were having a great time until her father came outside, looking angry and somewhat deranged—apparently his wife hadn't mentioned anything about the party before we arrived.

"The party's over. All of you, leave. Now!" he growled so loud that Vicki's mother heard him from inside their house.

"Walter, what the hell is wrong with you? Come back inside, now!" she said, racing outside and looking red with embarrassment.

He threw his cocktail glass on the patio, the broken pieces scattered all over the place.

"You better shut your mouth, Mia! Or do you want me to shut it for you?"

"I'm really sorry, girls, but you need to leave now," cried her mother, trying to avoid making things worse.

She took Vicki by the arm and pulled her inside as the rest of us left. I had never seen Vicki's father act like that, and I wondered why he was so mad. I went home and told my mother about it, and she said that Walter had lost his job a few weeks before and started drinking heavily. "Poor Mia," she mumbled, shaking her head. I thought about Vicki's absence for the last few months and I started to worry—she obviously wasn't staying home because she was sick. Later that day, she came to my house to explain what happened earlier. We sat on the porch, and when she bent forward to tie her shoelace, I noticed a big bruise on her back.

"Vicki, what is this?" I asked, touching the large purple bruise with my hand.

"Nothing," she assured me.

"Nothing? I don't believe you."

"Let it go, Ellen, please. Everything is fine."

"Okay, but I'm your best friend. You can talk to me about anything. You know that, right?"

I suspected her father had done this to her, but I couldn't figure out why. That night, as I laid in bed, I noticed that the closet door wasn't closed completely, even though I distinctly remembered shutting it earlier. Looking at it more closely, my heart skipped a beat when I saw a finger sticking out of the open crack. I tried not to scream because I didn't want to wake up Beth. Then, as I sat up, I saw a small hand emerge from the sliver, waving at me, while a high-pitched voice giggled behind the door. "Anna, if that's you, this isn't funny... you're scaring me!" I heard more giggles and then the door slammed closed abruptly. "Ellen, is the ghost here?" Beth asked, rubbing her eyes. "Mommy!" she screamed, as I put my hand over her mouth to muffle her call for help. My mother rushed into the room, "What's going on in here?" "Nothing, Mommy," I said, praying that she would believe me and leave, "Beth just had a bad dream." "No, I didn't!" Beth insisted. "Okay, that's enough, you two. Go to sleep," my mother said, closing the bedroom door. Beth rolled over, dismissing the incident, and I tried to do the same, but I found myself waking up every hour for the remainder of the night, afraid of seeing those fingers again.

• • •

Before I knew it, it was the start of the new school year. Vicki offered me her school uniform from the previous year—she gave me a lot of her clothes when they didn't fit her anymore. I noticed more and more bruises on her body and I became truly concerned. She seemed sad but hid it well. I rarely went to her house anymore, my mother said that it was probably better that way.

My eleventh birthday came and went like it was nothing. One month after school started, I got head lice. My teacher sent me home with an envelope containing instructions on how to get rid of it, and my mother was angry when I gave it to her. "God damnit, Ellen, now everyone in this family is going to have lice!" she snapped as she tossed the envelope to Catherine. She demanded that my sister go to the pharmacy and buy the proper shampoo and combs, and then she locked me in the bathroom. "I don't want the rest of us to get contaminated," she said with a disgusted look on her face. I wasn't sure what she meant by *contaminated*, but it didn't sound good, so I obeyed her and stayed in the bathroom until Catherine returned.

She applied the treatment in my hair, and then took me to the hairdresser down the street. She gave her a two-dollar bill and whispered something in her ear as both of them stared at me with sickened looks on their faces. I wished I could hear what she said. "Why are we at the hairdresser?" I asked Catherine when she came back over to me. "Because you have lice, and your hair needs to be trimmed," she responded. The thought of getting my hair cut worried me—I had long hair, which I kept in a ponytail most of time. The hairdresser wrapped a cape around me and spun the chair around, my back facing the mirror. She started working, and I heard a dull humming noise behind me. I was confused about why she wasn't just using scissors, but I let it go and sat quietly. Little did I know, my mother had called her before we got there and demanded that my head be shaved. When she turned me around and I saw myself in the mirror, I burst into tears. I looked like a boy! I think Catherine felt bad for me, I could see it in her face. "I'm sorry, Ellen, I didn't know Mom was going to tell her to shave it all. Don't worry, though, it will grow back before you know it." I cried all the way home, concealing my head with my hands, and then ran into the house and went directly to my room. My little brother and sister followed me, watching as I covered my head with a towel and cried myself to sleep.

I had never been this mad at my mother.

When I woke up the next morning, I saw a golden lock of hair on my dresser. My heart dropped—was that Anna's hair? I wondered how it got there and dashed to the kitchen to find out.

"Mommy, did you put this on my dresser?" I asked, showing her what I had just found moments earlier.

"What is this?" she asked, taking it from me and looking

genuinely perplexed. "Ellen, how did you get this? Did Anna's mother give it to you?"

"No. I just found it on my dresser this morning!"

She gave it back to me and said, "Ellen, if you went back to see Anna's mother and asked for it again, that's okay. But don't lie about it!" She moved back to the counter and continued making breakfast, while I stood in place and wondered why she never believed anything I said. I went back to my room and decided to store it in my desk, hidden and out of sight.

The next day, I dreaded going to school, afraid that people would make fun of me. When I got there, however, I was relieved to see that many other kids had their hair cut short too because of the lice outbreak, though only a few had it shaved completely. When I got home later, I asked my mother for a pair of her old nylons. "What for?" she asked, frowning and wondering what I was up to now. I told her I needed it for a game I was going to play with Vicki. "A game? What kind of game?" she asked dubiously. "We put a rubber ball in the leg of the nylons and swing it around," I lied. She didn't look too convinced, but she went along with it. "I'm going to Vicki's, I'll be back for dinner," I said, racing out the door before she could stop me.

When I reached the front yard and was certain that my mother couldn't see me, I put the nylons on my head and let the legs dangle over each of my shoulders. I'm sure it looked ridiculous, but it made me feel better—it was like I had hair again. I had outgrown my bicycle, so I walked confidently to Vicki's, ignoring the laughter of the people walking behind me. When I arrived at her house, I took a deep breath before I rang the bell, and Vicki's mother opened the door. "Wow, sweetie, why do you have nylons on your head?" she asked, laughing. "Because the hairdresser shaved off all my hair and I look like a boy now," I explained, tears pouring down my face. "Don't cry, it's okay. You should really take the nylons off though, it doesn't make it any better." We both laughed. Vicki heard us and came to the door—her hair had been cut too, but it wasn't shaved so she wasn't as unfortunate looking as me. I felt envious of her, just like I always was with Anna.

We sat in her backyard and talked for a while. The smell of fall warmed my heart. Suddenly, we heard Vicki's mother scream at the top of her lungs. She ran outside panting and then jumped the eight-foot fence that separated our houses into my yard, peering over at us and demanding that Vicki and I follow her. My mother heard the commotion and burst through the back door to see what was going on.

"Oh my God, Mia, what's happening?" she shrieked, looking alarmed.

"Kids, get inside right now! Walter is chasing me—with a knife!"

Everyone panicked and ran into my house, and my mother locked the screen door behind us. We were horrified when we saw Vicki's father jump the fence into our yard, carrying a sharp stainless-steel knife. He tripped and fell onto the grass, causing the knife to cut his hand, elevating his fury even more.

"Mia, get back here!" he yelled, as he pulled himself off the ground.

"Walter, calm down! Stop now! Before you do something that you'll regret for the rest of your life!" gasped my mother, shaking and anticipating the worst. She turned to Mia and urged her to call the police. Her hands were trembling so much that she had a hard time dialing the number on our rotary phone. Walter continued to growl for her to come outside, and when she refused, he stabbed his knife through the thin screen on our door. My mother, horrified that the small barrier between us and him was gone, promptly closed the main door and locked it. The police arrived a few minutes later and assessed the scene, before handcuffing Walter and putting him into the back of their squad car.

That was the last time I ever saw Vicki's father. Later, I heard my mother say that he had been sent to prison. Vicki was sad, but relieved because she and her mother didn't need to be living in fear anymore.

• • •

That year seemed to fly by and, before I knew it, I was turning twelve. I decided to celebrate at my friend Kathy's house because she also turned twelve on that day, and her parents had organized a birthday party for her. Vicki and I went to the mall to buy her a birthday present with the money we had saved from babysitting. I bought her a book, *The Witches of Worm*, about a lonely twelve-year-old girl who's convinced that the cats she finds are possessed by a witch. I knew Kathy would love it because she was fascinated by the supernatural. After the mall, we stopped at Vicki's house to wrap the presents, and I noticed a box already wrapped on the living room table. "This one is for you, Ellen, but you don't get to open it yet," Vicki said with a smirk, putting it in the bag with the other gifts.

Kathy's house looked inviting and was nicely decorated with streamers, balloons, and banners that said, "Happy Birthday!" We all gathered in the living room and sat in circle on the carpeted floor, and then Kathy's mother called us into to the kitchen. Her father stood there holding a birthday cake that was covered in candles, and everyone sang Happy Birthday to Kathy and me. Kathy's mother shouted enthusiastically, "Make a wish!" and we blew out the candles together. We went back to the living room after eating our cake, and Kathy gave me my present, a beautiful necklace made out of colourful beads, and I put it around my neck right away. Then, Vicki handed me a box that was covered in bright pink paper, and I began to unwrap it excitely. To my surprise, it was a Ouija board—I had always seen them advertised on the television—and I couldn't wait to try it out.

After the party, I went home and showed the gifts to my mother, but she wasn't as excited for me as I thought she would be. Instead, she looked extremely concerned.

"Oh my God, you cannot keep this thing, Ellen!" she shrieked, fearfully pointing to the board.

"Why?"

"Because it's evil. I don't want it here! I'm warning you, Ellen, you better not use it in this house or—"

"I know, I know. Or else God will punish me."

I took the Ouija board and hid it under my bed, ignoring what my mother said. How could it possibly be evil?

• • •

The next day, I realized that I forgot to give Kathy the birthday card I bought her, so I decided to bring it to her after dinner. When I arrived at her house, she invited me in for a leftover piece of cake from the party the day before, and we sat at the kitchen table and talked for a while. Time passed quickly, and I noticed it was dark outside. "I have to go, it's already nine o'clock. My parents are going to kill me!" I said as I got up from the table. Her mother offered to drive me home, but I declined—I enjoyed the walk.

I took the scenic route, a lovely trail by the farm with tall, majestic trees, and as I walked, enjoying the fresh air and silence, I heard a crackling sound behind me. I thought it might be an animal bustling about in the leaves, but I didn't see anything when I looked around. As I continued walking, the crunching sound got louder and closer. I jumped when I saw three boys leap out from behind the trees. One of them yelled, "Hey, where are you going?" as he moved towards me. I couldn't see their faces clearly, but I could tell that they were much taller and bigger than me. I started to run, scared to death, and when I tripped over a tree branch, I plunged to the ground. The other boy jumped on me and held me down, and in that moment, I wished my head was still shaved— maybe they would have left me alone if they thought I was a boy.

Then, one of them put his hand over my mouth to stop me from screaming out for help. "Keep your mouth shut, bitch!" he hollered, as his friend tightened his grip over each of my wrists. His hands felt rough, almost like sand paper, and he smelled like an ashtray. Then, the third boy tore my blouse open and pulled down my pants. I didn't understand what was happening, but I couldn't stop thinking that they were going to kill me.

I couldn't move. I couldn't scream. I couldn't breathe. I was helpless.

The third boy unzipped his pants and forced himself into me like a knife cutting into a piece of meat. He avoided looking at me, but I got a glimpse of his face, he had clear blue eyes and I also noticed a scar above his left eyebrow. After a few moments, his eyes rolled back as he exhaled and let out a disturbing moaning sound before he let the full weight of his body drop on top of me. I thought he had died, but then he moved off me and the boy who had his hand over my mouth came closer. I was in so much pain, I didn't think I could survive that again. I was about to pass out when I saw a butterfly fluttering over my head, and I prayed for Anna to help me. I let out a loud scream and immediately felt possessed by a power that turned my weakness into strength. In a demonic-like growl, I hissed, "Leave now or die." I pushed the boy off me with so much force that he went flying in the air and crashed onto the ground a few feet away.

"Shit let's go, guys, this girl is fucking possessed!" he shouted, pulling them as they fled.

In that moment, I had no doubt—Anna saved my life.

Writhing in pain, I rubbed my hand on the inside of my thigh and almost fainted at the sight of the blood. Shaking, I put my pants on and covered myself with my jacket, leaving my ripped blouse on the ground. I had no idea monsters like this existed. My mother had never talked about sex with me before—was it supposed to be so violent?

Was this a punishment from God?

I made it home even though I was in agonizing pain. When I opened the front door, my mother heard it squeak, and came to the hall to yell at me for being late.

"Jesus Christ, what the hell happened to you?" she asked, seeing that I was covered in dirt and blood.

I threw myself into her arms, and she held me, it felt comforting.

"Ellen, stop crying for a minute. You need to tell me what happened," she insisted, starting to get more worked up.

My father heard us and rushed to the front door. He thought I had been run over by a car.

"What on earth happened to you, Ellen? Why did you come home so late? Where have you been?"

"I was... attacked..." I whispered, unable to catch my breath.

"Attacked? What do you mean attacked? Who did this to you? Where were you?" he asked, anger flaring up in his eyes.

"Boys... three boys... on the trail..."

Both my mother and father looked horrified. I didn't have to explain, they figured it out right away. My mother took me to the bathroom and saw the blood between my legs, and then ran a hot bath.

"You shouldn't be walking on a dark path alone, Ellen," she murmured, continuing to softly wash my body and trying to conceal her tears.

I know that now.

I put my pajamas on, and my father sat me at the kitchen table to ask me an endless string of questions. Even though I took a bath and changed my clothes, I couldn't stop shaking—nothing could make this situation better.

"I'm going to find those boys, and they're going to be really sorry when I do," he exploded. His face was red with anger, but I could see a glimmer of sadness and remorse in his eyes because he wasn't able to protect me.

"John, I think you need to take her to the hospital, she's bleeding," my mother said, coming up behind my chair.

He carried me to the car, still in my pajamas. The hospital was only ten minutes away, but the drive seemed like it took forever. When we got there, we were asked to wait in the emergency room. It took an hour before the doctor came to see me. He asked what happened, but I couldn't get a word out so my father explained everything. The doctor examined me—the bruises were visible all over my body. "I won't examine her down there," the doctor whispered, "I don't want to add to her trauma." Then, he asked my dad whether I started my period yet, and he told him no and that I was only twelve years old.

My period? What is that?

"You'll need to report this to the police immediately, Mr. Taylor," the doctor ordered, then he and my father exchanged a few words as I put my pajamas back on and we left.

My parents called the police as soon as we got home, and two large men in uniforms arrived at around midnight. They asked so many questions it made my head spin—I just wanted to go to sleep.

"You need to find those bastards and throw them in jail!" my father said, infuriated.

"We will do everything we can to find them, Mr. Taylor," the police officer said. "Unfortunately, we don't have much to go on because your daughter didn't see their faces clearly. Please call us back if she remembers anything else." Why were they talking about me as though I wasn't even there? I went to bed and cried all night, unable to comprehend what had just happened, and I didn't yet realize that the events of that night would affect me for the rest of my life.

. . .

That weekend, Vicki called me to tell me that her mother had gone out and insisted that I come over so she could make sure I was okay. Before I left, I pulled the Ouija board out from under my bed, put it in a bag, and then raced to her house. When I got there, she gave me a hug and said that she was so sorry about what happened. It felt good to know that I wasn't alone, and sharing this horrific event with her made us closer. Then, we went to her bedroom, closed the blinds, and lit up the room with a few candles that smelled like lavender and vanilla. We sat on the floor facing each other with our knees touching and eagerly read the game's instructions. Then, placing the board on our laps with our fingers touching the planchette, I worked up the courage to ask the first question.

"Spirit, are you with us?" I whispered, listening intently for an answer.

The pointer didn't move, so I waited ten seconds and asked again, more resolute this time.

"Spirit, give us a sign that you're with us."

The pointer began to glide slowly to the word YES at the top left corner of the board. Vicki gave me a wide-eyed look that showed her terror and suggested her hidden suspicion that I had dragged the pointer across the board just to scare her. I was nervous but also curious, so I asked another question.

"Spirit, is there a ghost present in this room?"

Then, the pointer shifted down slightly on the board before it moved its way up to the word *YES* again.

"Spirit, what is the ghost's name?"

It started moving rapidly across the board, and we struggled to decipher what it spelled: *Z-O-Z-O.*

"I don't like this, Ellen. I have a bad feeling. I think we should stop," Vicki squeaked, covering her eyes with her hands.

"Don't be scared, Vicki. You're not in danger," I promised, placing my hand on her arm to comfort her.

I took a deep breath and continued with my questions.

"Spirit, where is Zozo right now?"

Suddenly, the planchette jolted around the board over random letters, making no sense at all, and then moved to each of the board's four corners. Vicki and I looked at each other in terror, we couldn't believe what happened next—the pointer flew across the room and hit the wall.

"Holy shit! Okay, that's enough! We're done with this, Ellen. This board is possessed!" Vicki shouted, tossing the board off her lap and standing up.

"Wait! Did you hear that?" I asked, focusing on an unlit corner of her bedroom.

"What? I didn't hear anything! Ellen, stop trying to scare me. This isn't funny anymore!" Vicki yelled, looking as if she was about to burst into tears.

Hesitant to discover what it was, but unwilling to look away, I approached the corner of the room. As I got closer, I heard a loud growl as a dark figure appeared in the corner, staring back at me. I quickly glanced over at Vicki, but she continued to look confused about what I was talking about—how could she not see or hear it? I immediately blew out the candles and pulled the blinds open, my heart racing.

"Your mother was right, Ellen. Ouija is evil!"

I picked up the board and placed the planchette on *GOODBYE OUIJA*—the instructions said that this was an essential step before putting the game away—and then we decided to go for a walk to try to calm ourselves down.

"Honestly, Ellen, you need to get rid of that board right now," she insisted as we walked down the road.

"Yeah, I will," I replied nonchalantly.

"I'm serious, Ellen, this is *frickin'* scary!"

I went home and hid the board in my closet. I wasn't quite ready to get rid of it just yet—who knows, maybe I would have use for it again. The next day, I couldn't stop thinking about Zozo—what did that mean? I had to find out, so I went to the library to do some research. I came across an old, dusty book that described Zozo as a demon that preys on the souls of the innocent after it stalks and torments them in the night. Maybe my mother was right to warn me about this Ouija board, I thought, not knowing just how evil the spirit we had evoked really was.

CHAPTER SIX
NEW BEGINNINGS

Before I knew it, I was starting high school. It didn't live up to all the hype—some people even went so far as to say that it was the best years of their lives, but I didn't agree with this at all. I wasn't a fan of the cliques and popularity contests. I was a loner and didn't like any attention from anyone, especially the boys. Shortly after I started school, I finally met a boy I liked. During the second week, I was running down the hallway trying to get to class on time and I ran right into him, causing him to lose his balance and drop his books all over the floor.

"I'm so sorry!" I said, turning bright red and apologizing repeatedly as I picked up the books one by one.

"It's okay, don't worry about it," he said, smiling at me.

He looked deep into my eyes as we both got up off the floor, but I didn't want him to see me blushing, so I quickly walked away even though he was running to try to catch up to me.

"Hey, I'm Paul by the way," he said, shaking my hand nervously.

"Nice to meet you, Paul. If you'll excuse me, I have to go now. I'm late for class."

"Wait! What are you doing during the lunch break?" His face turned red, I could tell he was shy too.

"Well, I usually eat my lunch outside under the willow tree."

"Do you mind if I join you?"

"Um, if you want to... sure," I said meekly.

"I'll be there. But first, aren't you going to tell me your name?"

"Oh sorry, I'm Ellen. Ellen Taylor."

"See you at lunch, Ellen Taylor," he said, smiling as we both parted ways.

As I sat in class, I couldn't stop thinking about what had just happened. This was the first time a boy had ever been nice to me, and it made me feel like I was as light as air.

"Ellen, are you with us?" my teacher said, snapping his fingers to jolt me out of my daydream. "I'm still waiting for an answer, Miss Ellen," he persisted, looking thoroughly unimpressed.

"I'm sorry... can you repeat the question please?"

"Stay with the program, Ellen," he said angrily, calling on another student.

My lunch break couldn't have come soon enough. I ran to meet Paul outside at the willow tree and after we sat down I instantly started to feel at ease. We didn't run out of things to talk about, and before I knew it, the bell rang and it was time to go back to class. We started meeting under the willow tree every day, talking about everything from our classes and gossip about our classmates, to our favourite books and places to hang out.

Just a couple of weeks later he kissed me, and over the next few weeks we fell in love, which was a first for both of us. Paul was tall and handsome, and I loved his big blue eyes, plump lips, and slick brown shoulder length hair. But most of all, I loved how sensitive and kind he was—and the fact that he was such an amazing kisser didn't hurt either! It didn't even matter that he was two years older than me, and I was confident that, even though he would graduate high school before me, we could make it work.

Paul lived twenty minutes from my house, and we saw each other every day after school and on the weekends. But that all changed one day when my dad announced that we were moving to a house in the country, almost an hour away from the city—I guess it's true that nothing lasts forever. My entire world collapsed around me. I went to my room and cried for hours, trying to decide how to break the news to Paul. I waited until the end of the week, when we went to our favourite coffee shop after seeing a movie. I started sobbing when I told him, barely able to get the words out. Paul reached his hands across the table and laid them over mine.

"Don't cry, it's going to be okay. I'm getting my driver's license soon, so it will be easy to come see you. We can make this work, Ellen, I promise," he said calmly, always knowing exactly what to say to make me feel better.

"I love you so much, Paul. I'm so scared of losing you!"

"You won't, Ellen, I promise. Don't worry."

We sat in the coffee shop for two hours, making a detailed plan about when we could see each other. I was determined to make this work—how hard could a long-distance relationship be?

• • •

Our new four-bedroom house was a bit nicer than my previous one, and it was also much more spacious. My sister Catherine got her own room and I had to share with Beth again, but at least this time each of us had our own bed. I didn't like that the house was so far away from everything, not even city buses ran in our area. Paul came to see me on the weekends, riding his ten-speed bike, and we eagerly awaited the opportunity to get our driver's licenses. I started a part-time job at a fast food restaurant near my house and I gradually began to save money for driving lessons.

One night, as I walked home after my shift, I felt an eerie presence. It was as if someone was following me, but I couldn't see anything when I turned back to look. Dismissing it, I continued walking until I felt something touch my arm. I jumped, the hair on the back of my neck raising, and plucked up the courage to look behind me again. This time, the blank void that was there before was filled by a dark shadow, moving quickly towards me. I didn't wait for it to come any closer before I sprinted home as fast as my feet could carry me. When I rushed through the front door, my mother was in the kitchen washing the dishes and she looked at me with confusion.

"What's wrong, Ellen? Is everything okay?"

I ignored her and ascended the stairs to my room, and tried to convince myself that my mind was playing tricks on me. It must have just been a shadow or an animal, I thought. But, what touched my arm?

That night, I dreamt about the house with the long hallway and seven doors. I found it bizarre that the boy in my dream never seemed to age—he was forever seven years old. No matter how hard I tried to stay asleep, I continued to wake up right before he could unlock the seventh door, and finding out what was behind it became my obsession.

• • •

My friend Kathy recommended a psychic that one of her friends had been to, so I made an appointment for that Friday evening to satisfy my curiosity.

"I don't understand why you're wasting your money on this, Ellen," Catherine said, giving me a judgmental look after I asked her to drive me there.

"Will you take me or not?" I pressed, knowing that she would agree eventually.

"Fine, if I have to," she said, rolling her eyes.

On the way to the psychic's house, I checked the address on the piece of paper Kathy gave me. The house number was seventy-seven—was this a sign or just a coincidence? I scratched my head in disbelief. Catherine parked in the driveway, and I inspected the house. The exterior looked gloomy and tired with its chipped paint on the white shingles and the shagged roof showing its age. The flickering of the candles in the front window made it look even more ominous, but I suppressed my apprehension and got out of the car. I knocked on the door twice, and then a woman glanced at me through the cracked window before opening it. She looked just as old as her house with her thin white hair, wrinkled skin, and droopy eyes. She smiled at me, revealing her yellow teeth.

"Come in," she said, in a sonorous voice.

"Hi, is it okay if my sister waits for me inside?"

"Of course, come on in."

I entered slowly, taking in the smell of cigarette smoke mixed with burning incense.

"I'm Lucille."

Her name has seven letters in it! There's no way this was a coincidence, I thought.

She pointed to a small alcove by the living room next to the entrance. Everything in the small area was red, from the carpet to the walls and the furniture.

"You can wait right here," she said to Catherine, who looked at me with her disparaging stare, almost as if she was about to burst out laughing. Ignoring my sister's disapproval, I followed Lucille into an adjacent room. As we entered, two cats rushed through the door, meowing, as if something had scared them.

"Have a seat, dear, and tell me why you're here."

Sitting down at an old wooden table, I looked around the intimidating room. It was the exact opposite of the red room in the hallway—the walls and furniture were all black and the only light came from the dancing flames of a few candles placed around the table. I felt like I was a prisoner locked away in a dungeon, but I took a deep breath and tried to decide where to begin.

"Umm... I'd like to know if I have any spirits around me," I muttered, almost in a whisper.

"Tell me more."

I didn't want to give away the details. After all, she's a psychic—shouldn't she know everything already?

"That's all, really."

"Okay then," she said, gazing back at me with a strange look on her face.

She leaned against the table, putting her hands over mine and closing her eyes. She started chanting and then opened her eyes again and looked straight at me.

"Who is that?" she asked.

"Pardon? Who are you talking about?"

"The young girl next to you."

I turned my head sharply, but didn't see anything.

"She's wearing a pink dress."

My heart leapt out of my chest, not because I was afraid, but because I was excited that Anna was still close to me even after all this time.

"That's my friend Anna, she's a ghost."

"Well, she's not alone, dear."

"What do you mean?"

"There's a woman with her."

Who could that woman be? Why had I never seen her before?

"Do you know her?" she asked, revealing a flash of uneasiness in her eyes.

"I know who the girl is, but not the woman," I answered, afraid of what she would say next.

"The woman… she is talking about a little boy…"

"A little boy?"

"Yes, dear. She says they are related."

"They are? How old is the boy?"

"She says he's seven."

"You don't need to be afraid of them. They will protect you," she said reassuringly.

It was obvious that the girl she described was Anna and the boy was the one who appeared in my dream of the hallway, but I had no idea how they were connected. I felt even more confused than before. The next thing I knew our hour was up and I had to leave. I wanted to find out more, but Lucille said that she had another client waiting and told me I could schedule another reading. I took a twenty-dollar bill out of my purse and gave it to her and then exited the room to get Catherine. "It's about time!" she said, the red of the room reflecting off her skin. On the ride home, she kept probing me to find out what the psychic said. I told her that Lucille was somewhat vague, which prompted an immediate, "I told you! You wasted your money!" from my sister. She wouldn't have believed me if I told her the truth anyway.

• • •

A few weeks later, I finally got my driver's license, which was useless because I didn't have a car yet and Catherine wouldn't let me drive hers. She said that she'd sell it to me when I had enough money, so I saved every penny I earned to buy it. After school that Friday, Paul picked me up in his father's car, and we went to the movies. After it was over, he drove me straight home, which confused me because we usually went for coffee afterwards. When we got to my place, he pulled into my driveway and kept the engine running, looking restless and in a hurry. He gave me a quick peck on the cheek before I got out of the car, and said, "I love you sweetheart," with a hint of sadness in his voice. I sensed something wasn't right, so I got back in the front seat and closed the door.

"Is everything okay, Paul?"

"I didn't want to talk about it tonight, Ellen, but I guess we should…"

"What is it? You're scaring me."

"I was accepted to the university out west. I'll be moving there in two weeks."

My heart dropped.

"You're moving? In two weeks?" I said, unable to comprehend what he was telling me.

"Don't cry, sweetheart, we will still be able see each other. I'll come back every other weekend or so."

"But it's so far away, Paul. Everyone always says that long distance relationships never work."

"Don't listen to that, Ellen. We're different."

How could he be so certain?

I got out of the car, tears streaming down my face, and slammed the door without saying goodbye. He rolled down his window, "Ellen, please don't be like that." I didn't reply. When I got inside, my mother was at the entrance, waiting for me. She asked what happened and if I was alright, but I couldn't look at her and simply told her that I was just tired. "I think there's more to it, Ellen, I know you better than that." Fighting to hold back my tears, I didn't reply and went straight to bed.

. . .

When Paul moved two weeks later, I started to miss him as soon as he left. We talked on the phone every other day, and it seemed like he was happy and settling into his new life. This made me glad, but I also experienced such immense sadness because he didn't seem to miss me as much as I missed him. As the weeks passed, we started getting more distant. I couldn't take the chasm between us any longer, so I asked when he would be back, but he danced around the question before telling me he had too much school work and wouldn't be able to travel for a few weeks. This meant that he would miss my seventeenth birthday. The heartbreak I felt was indescribable, and it made me not want to celebrate it at all.

When Vicki found out, she insisted that we celebrate my birthday at a pub near her place to help me forget about my troubles with Paul. We used fake IDs to get in and drank far too much before leaving the bar around midnight. On our way back to her place, we stumbled through the yard of the school we went to when we were young. Feeling dizzy and tired, we decided to take a break and sit in the schoolyard. We must have accidentally fallen asleep, and I woke up in the morning to a kid tapping me gently on my side with his foot. I heard him say to his friend, "Bobby, I think she's dead!" I opened my eyes and sat straight up, groaning because of my splitting headache, which prompted the boys to run away. Hearing the commotion, Vicki woke up, putting her hand on her pounding head, and said, "Oh my God, Ellen, I can't believe we slept here all night. We're in so much trouble. My mother is probably worried sick!" I immediately began fearing what my own mother would do if she found out that we didn't return to Vicki's last night. We ran all the way to her house, even though we knew it was too late to avoid getting in trouble. When we arrived, Vicki's mother was at the door, looking relieved and upset.

"Jesus, Vicki, what happened? Where were you? I called the police, I thought you had been kidnapped or something!"

"I'm sorry, Mom, we fell asleep in the schoolyard..."

"In the schoolyard? Why? I can't believe this. We'll talk about this later, young lady. Ellen, get in the car, I'll drive you home."

I got an earful from my mother as soon as I walked in the door, and she grounded me for a month. Knowing that talking back or trying to explain myself would just make the situation worse, I quietly went upstairs and took a bath before I went to bed. As I was dozing into a deep sleep, my body started to vibrate like an electrical current was running through me. Suddenly, I couldn't move my arms or legs, and I felt as though I was being lifted out of my body and floating above it. I began flying around my room, like a disoriented bird bumping into walls. This must be what death felt like, I thought.

When I finally came back into my body, I was out of breath, gasping like I was drowning. I looked around and noticed that the picture frame on my wall had fallen to the floor and shattered, and there were two handprints on the mirror of my dresser. I started shaking uncontrollably, unable to understand what just happened to me. I couldn't let these strange things happen anymore, I had to find answers.

Later that day, I asked Catherine to drive me to the library in town so I could take out a book on astral projections. When she asked why I picked that book, I told her that someone at school asked me to get it for her. I knew she didn't believe me. "You're weird, Ellen," she said, rolling her eyes and shaking her head.

That same day, Catherine let me drive her car for the first time, so I drove to the cemetery. Anna had been gone for ten years, which I found hard to imagine—it felt like yesterday that I was crouched down beside her lifeless body, trying as hard as I could to get her to wake up. I stopped at the flower shop on my way to get a pink rose, just as I did every year, and when I got to the cemetery, I was surprised that there weren't fresh flowers on her grave. I found out later that Anna's mother had died two months before—people said of a broken heart—and her father sold the house and moved to another city.

I understood how it was possible for someone to die of a broken heart. That's how I felt when my life turned upside down after my relationship with Paul ended. He stopped calling and writing, and not long after I heard he was dating a girl he met at school. I felt like I would never be happy again, and this feeling was more painful than anything I'd ever experienced. I empathized with Anna's mother and, just for a split second, I envied her because she didn't have to feel such pain and loss any longer.

• • •

When I turned eighteen, Vicki and I went to the same pub as the year before, but this time with real IDs. When we got to the door, looking proud because we were of age, the doorman looked at our IDs and said, "So, all this time I let you in, you were under age?" I turned red, embarrassed and scared that we could get in trouble, but he laughed and let us through the door. We listened to music by a local band and drank a couple of beers, and then Vicki surprised me with a gift, a classic white-faced watch with a black leather band. "Now you have no more excuses for being late, best friend," she said, laughing. Little did she know, I already owned a watch, but I thought it was defective, so I never wore it—for some reason the time always froze at 7:07.

Vicki's mother picked us up at the end of the evening and she drove me home. I decided that I wasn't ready go to inside right away, so I went to the backyard and laid down on the grass, looking up at the starry sky, thinking about Anna and wondering if her mother was with her. Then, a light breeze carrying the fragrance of roses washed over me. "Anna, I know you're here," I said, feeling comforted. I closed my eyes for a few seconds and, when I reopened them, I saw three shadows standing directly in front of me. I sat upright and looked again, and they were still there, completely still.

I got up and ran inside the house, where my mother was reading in the kitchen. "What's wrong? You look like you've just seen a ghost."

"Three of them—to be precise," I said, immediately regretting it. She never believed me and probably never would, I came to accept that. I went to my room, where Beth was already asleep, and put on my pyjamas and went to bed. When I turned over to my side, I saw the same three shadows standing motionless at the door.

I ignored them—this was starting to happen more often. Maybe I should just get used to it, I thought.

CHAPTER SEVEN
DARK MATTER

After I graduated high school, I decided to take a break from school and work full-time at a local cable company, which helped me save enough money to buy my sister's car and move out of my parent's house. I was so excited for the change, especially because Vicki and I planned on moving in together. We found a spacious apartment close to where we worked—and coincidently the apartment number was seven hundred and seventeen and located on the seventh floor.

We moved in on the first of July with the help of my two brothers, and Vicki's mother gave us some dishes, pots and pans, towels, blankets, and many other household items so that we didn't have to spend too much money. Vicki brought her bedroom set, and I kept my twin bed and dresser. I picked up a second job as a waitress on the weekends to pay for my half of the rent, while Vicki worked every Thursday until Sunday because she had school during the week. I loved the freedom of being away from home and not having to answer to my parents, it truly felt like a new beginning.

After a few weeks, we were all settled in and had established a routine. I enjoyed spending time alone doing whatever I wanted while Vicki was at work, and I started learning how to play the guitar—I got it from my brother James when he bought himself a new one. One day, as I sat on the floor trying to master a new song, my vision blurred and everything went dark. When I regained consciousness, it was 9pm, and I was wrapped tightly in a blanket from my bed, lying on the sofa, my guitar on the floor on the other side of the room. I untangled myself from the blanket and went to see if anything looked different in any of the other rooms. Everything seemed to be intact, so I turned on each light in the apartment and went back to the living room, deciding I was just needlessly scaring myself and that there was a perfectly reasonable explanation for all of this.

As soon as I sat down on the couch, all the lights began to flicker before shutting off completely and plunging the room into darkness. I started panicking and, when I looked around, I noticed that my guitar wasn't on the floor anymore, but it was put back in its case, and the blanket that was wrapped around me had disappeared from the couch. The room became ice-cold and completely silent. "Anna, if you're doing this, you need to stop!" I pleaded, unable to understand why she would want to scare me like this. Suddenly, all the lights came back on and everything was back to normal.

Was I going crazy?

I sat motionless in the living room, trying to rationalize what just happened. Vicki arrived home an hour later, immediately noticing that something was wrong when she walked through the door.

"Ellen, you're as white as a ghost. Are you okay?" she asked, frowning and looking worried.

"Were you in the apartment earlier? Around six o'clock?" I asked, ignoring her question.

"No, I went straight to work after school. Why?"

"Something really strange happened. If I told you, you probably wouldn't believe me."

"Try me! You can tell me anything, Ellen," she said reassuringly.

I went through every detail with her, step by step, but neither one of us could find a plausible explanation. We both agreed that it would have been impossible for me to take the blanket from my bed and put the guitar back in its case without realizing that I had done it. Someone else must have been there.

I slept in Vicki's' room that night, terrified and worried that all the horrors over the last few years had followed me to my new beginning.

. . .

Vicki had been dating a man named Mike for the last year, and one day she came home and announced that they were engaged. I felt a mix of different emotions. On the one hand, I was so happy for her because she had found someone to share her life with, but on the other hand I was worried that she would move out and leave me all alone. As we sat down for dinner one night, I could feel an awkward tension between us and decided to clear the air.

"Vicki, what's your plan now that you're engaged?" I asked, afraid to hear her answer.

"Well, I was going to bring it up tomorrow, Ellen, but I guess we can talk about it now. Mike asked me to move in with him, and I really want to, but I also don't want to leave you stranded and mad at me," she replied, hesitantly.

"It's okay, don't worry. I'll just have to find a smaller apartment." I didn't really have a choice, I thought.

"I won't move for a few months until our lease is up, though, so there's still time," she reasoned, trying to make the situation better.

All this talk of marriage and seeing Vicki's sparkly engagement ring made me miss Paul. I hadn't heard from him in such a long time, even though I knew he must have come home to visit his parents at some point in the last few months. My heart ached just thinking that he never bothered to get in touch.

The next day, I went to the building manager's office to give him our final notice, and then headed out to see some apartments close by. I found a charming one-bedroom unit on the second floor of a two-story home, just a short walk from work. I felt excited, but also nervous to be living entirely on my own.

On moving day, my older brother helped me carry all the

furniture from our old apartment—Vicki was nice enough to leave everything for me—and we spent the afternoon painting. I really wanted to make this place my own, so I chose a rosy-pink colour for my bedroom and a light yellow for the living room, and stenciled a butterfly on the kitchen wall. It looked perfect.

Two days after I moved in, I heard a loud knock on my door that immediately made me jump. I got up from the couch and nervously looked through the curtains, hoping that whoever was out there wouldn't spot me. On the other side of the door stood my landlord's wife, who was tall, thin, and blonde—she looked just like the Barbie I got for Christmas when I was younger. Feeling a sense of relief, I opened the door.

"Hi, Ellen. Sorry, I didn't mean to wake you. I made some fresh coffee and thought you might like a cup," she said, smiling at me and holding a large mug in her left hand.

"That's so nice, thank you!" I responded, somewhat surprised at her warm demeanour and thoughtfulness.

"I'm Donna by the way."

"Nice to meet you, Donna," I replied shaking her hand.

"If you ever need anything at all, don't hesitate to ask."

"Thanks, Donna," I said, feeling relieved and thinking that, just maybe, I wasn't entirely alone.

• • •

A month later, I decided it was time to pursue a new career, so I joined a law firm as a legal secretary and enrolled in night school to get my Paralegal Assistant certificate. Suddenly, I felt like I had a clear and defined goal and was motivated to do anything it took to achieve it. I invited Vicki over for dinner to tell her my exciting news. When she arrived, I hugged her tightly, feeling like I hadn't seen her in forever, and took her on a tour of the apartment.

"This place is beautiful, Ellen. I love all the different colours!"

We sat at my small kitchen table to eat the spaghetti and meatballs I prepared, but as we started talking more I noticed that she wasn't her usual positive and joyful self.

"How are things with Mike? I feel so out of the loop, you have to tell me everything!" I asked, lightly pressing her, hoping that she would tell me what was really on her mind.

"Everything is good..." she responded, unconvincingly.

"Just good? What's wrong, Vicki?"

"Well, I'm still adjusting I guess. Mike is... well... he's—"

"Come on, Vicki, you know you can tell me anything. What's going on?" I said, placing my hand on her shoulder, which made her start to cry.

"Well, Mike is a very jealous and controlling man and he has a really bad temper. But he must just act this way because he loves me so much... that must be it."

"Vicki, has he ever hurt you? You can tell me the truth."

She paused, then muttered, "Well, last week... I think I made him angry because he pulled me by my hair... and then threw me to the ground... and then he kicked me in the stomach..." She looked embarrassed, and I could tell that she was afraid of what my reaction would be.

"What? Oh my God, Vicki! Why would he do that? You can't let him hurt you like that!" I was completely shocked. Mike always seemed so timid and soft-spoken, it was hard to believe that he could turn into such a monster.

"He doesn't mean to hurt me, he just gets carried away sometimes. I know he loves me—"

"How can you say he loves you?!" I interrupted, feeling frustrated by her naivety. "Come on, Vicki. If he really loved you, he would never hurt you!"

"I know, but he's just stressed. His job—"

"Okay, stop it Vicki," I interjected again, unable to take these rationalizations any longer. "There are no excuses for this behaviour! Did you ever see this side of him when you were dating?"

"No, of course not. If I had, I wouldn't have moved in with him."

"It's not too late. You can move back with me."

I did everything to convince her to leave him, but no matter how hard I tried, she insisted on giving him another chance.

I guess life is full of surprises—even if they're not always good.

CHAPTER EIGHT
BE CAREFUL WHAT YOU WISH FOR

I started taking the bus to get to night school because it was easier and much less expensive than taking my car. On my way after work one day, I looked up and saw a young man get on, quickly pay his fare, and sit beside me, even though the bus was almost completely empty.

"Hi there, I'm Jack," he said, smiling at me with a cheerful grin.

I muttered a quick hello back, but couldn't look at him in the eye. I hated awkward situations like this, especially because he wouldn't stop staring at me as he scanned my body like I was a piece of meat. Vicki often reminded me that I was popular with boys, saying that she envied my well-proportioned body shape and my gold-speckled hazel eyes. But I never liked the attention.

"What's your name?" he asked.

"Do we know each other?"

"Why? Do I have to know someone to say hello?"

I didn't answer him, hoping he would give up and stop talking to me.

"Cat got your tongue?" he tried again.

"Ellen. My name is Ellen," I said finally. Maybe now he would leave me alone.

"Ellen, that's a nice name. Has anyone ever told you how pretty you are, Ellen?"

I turned my head the other way, ignoring this compliment. My stop couldn't come soon enough. As the bus approached the school, I tried to stand up, but his knees were blocking my way out.

"Excuse me. This is my exit, I need to get out," I said, unimpressed.

He paused for a second too long, then flashed a smirk and said, "Well, Ellen, I hope to see you again sometime soon."

I pretended like I was brushing him off, but I secretly liked this playful banter—so much so that I had a hard time concentrating in class that evening. While I didn't know anything about this young man, there was something about him that piqued my curiosity. I kept wondering where or when we might meet again, and every time I got on the bus I held my breath in anticipation. After a month of anxiously waiting—and almost giving up hope—my heart fluttered when he climbed onto the bus and walked directly to my seat.

"Hi, can I sit here?" he asked.

I nodded.

"It's good to see you again."

This time, I smiled back and looked at him.

"Ellen, right?"

"Yes, and you are Jack, correct?" I turned bright red because of my complete inability to make small talk. "Do you live around here?" I continued, trying to break the ice.

"Why? Would you like to come over?" he smirked.

"No, just curious."

"I don't live too far from here. You?"

"Um… I live with my parents," I lied, not knowing why.

"Hey, I'd love it if you'd give me your phone number, Ellen. Would that be alright?" he asked, giving away a glimmer of vulnerability for the first time.

I didn't know if I should give it to him. After all, he was a stranger.

"Don't worry, I'm not a stalker," he assured me, as if reading my mind. "I just thought we could maybe go out for a drink or dinner one day."

He dug a piece of paper and a pen out of his bag and handed it to me. I wrote my number down, but immediately regretted it—how could I trust this boy?

"Thank you. I'll call you soon, Ellen," he said, getting up and moving to the exit door.

• • •

A few days later, I was lying on my bed reading a book when the smell of an extinguished candle filled the room. I was confused because I hadn't lit any candles before I started reading. As I scanned the room, I saw a man and a woman standing next to my bed, wearing white knee-length laboratory coats and staring straight at me. I struggled to maintain eye contact, my heart pounding so fast that I began to hyperventilate. My mind urged my body to run or scream for help, but I was frozen. The man looked pale and very thin and was waving around a syringe in his right hand as he quietly conversed with the woman, who had a threatening look plastered across her face. When they stopped talking, she gave me a sharp glare and approached me, putting her right hand on my forehead and brushing my hair back. As she did this, the man leaned over me, his white coat dangling over my face, and pierced the top of my head with his needle, the excruciating pain radiated through my skull.

I couldn't talk. I couldn't scream. I couldn't move. I was helpless.

I heard the man and the woman whisper something again, but their words made no sense to me. It felt like a lifetime before he finally pulled the needle out of my head, and then she placed her hand over my heart, which instantly calmed me down. Then they disappeared and suddenly I could move my body again. I touched the top of my head, trying to make the numbness go away, and then I looked at my finger, stained with blood. I sat there staring blankly, trying to figure out who those people were and how they got there—and, perhaps more importantly, what they wanted.

I slowly got out of bed and turned on all the lights as I looked in every corner of my apartment. I lowered myself onto the couch, scanning everything one last time, but nothing appeared to be out of place. I must have fallen asleep because, when I woke up, light was cascading through the windows and my alarm clock was beeping in my bedroom. I staggered to my room to shut it off, then took a shower, got dressed, and went to work, like nothing ever happened.

As I walked through the doors of my office and sat down at my desk, my colleague Linda immediately noticed I wasn't my usual self.

"Good morning, Ellen. Did you sleep okay? You look tired today," she said. The dark circles under my eyes must have given me away. "Let's get a coffee, it looks like you could use one," she insisted, as if coffee would help.

"Linda, if I share something personal with you, do you promise not to judge me?"

"Of course not. What's going on?"

I told her what happened, and she looked at me in disbelief, just like everyone else did so many times before.

"You believe me, right?" I asked.

"I do! But even you must admit that this is pretty bizarre!" she responded, plastering on an over exaggerated smile to convince me that she didn't think I was completely crazy.

I showed her the mark where the man pierced my head with the needle, hoping that maybe this would convince her that I wasn't making this up.

"Yikes! You have a bloody scab there. You must have bumped your head while you were sleeping. You should see a doctor!"

If this didn't convince her, nothing would, so I got back to work and kept to myself for the rest of the day, hoping that I would find some rational explanation for what happened the night before.

By the end of the day, the last thing I felt like doing was going to school, so I went home and made myself some chicken soup. My mother was right, there is something so incredibly comforting about chicken soup. I clicked on the television and got lost in a movie and finally started to get some much-needed rest. Just as I was dozing off, the phone rang, so I picked it up to see who could be calling at this hour.

"Hi, Ellen, it's Jack. I hope it's not too late to be calling."

I didn't feel like talking to him, this day was so long and I just wanted it to be over, so I told him I had a friend over and couldn't talk.

"Got it, no problem. I was just calling to ask you out for a drink tomorrow night."

It took a second for it to register—he was asking me out on a date! I debated whether I should go. Sure, I was intrigued by him, but did I have time for this right now?

"Ellen? You still there?" he asked, breaking me out of my silent deliberation.

"Okay… yeah, I guess so. But I have class tomorrow evening, so it would have to be after nine o'clock," I said, finally giving in. He seemed nice, and God knows I needed the distraction.

"Nine sounds perfect! Looking forward to it!" he answered excitedly, telling me the address and then hanging up quickly so that I wouldn't change my mind.

• • •

The next day, as I got ready for my date, I felt a mix of nervousness and excitement. When I arrived at the bar, I stayed in my car for a few minutes, trying to convince myself that I shouldn't worry and that this was going to be fun. I could see Jack inside, seated at a wooden booth that was adjacent to the large glass window, and I looked down, feeling embarrassed already. When I glanced up, Jack had spotted me and started waving as he got up to meet me outside. It was too late to back out now, so I slowly climbed out of the car and walked over to meet him.

"Ellen, it's great to see you!" he exclaimed as we walked inside.

"I see you started drinking without me," I said playfully, noticing a pitcher of beer on the table.

I hadn't planned on drinking, but I figured it would help me relax, so I took a glass from him and sipped it slowly. Over the next two hours, we filled the air with casual conversation, and I began to feel strangely comfortable with him. After he paid the bill and walked me to my car, he asked if he could see me again, before leaning forward to kiss me on the cheek. I said yes, even though I still wasn't completely sure, and got into my car and left.

When I arrived home, I ripped a sheet of paper out of my school notebook and traced a vertical line in the middle of it, writing what I liked about Jack on one side and what I didn't like about him on the other. Just as I suspected, I ended up with more likes than dislikes, and this made my heart flutter with excitement. Then the doorbell chimed—did Jack follow me home? I opened the door and saw Donna standing on the other side.

"Donna, hi!" I said, feeling relieved.

"Sorry to bother you this late, Ellen, but you left your head-lights on. I didn't want you to wake up to a dead battery tomorrow morning."

"Oh, thank you so much for letting me know. I'll go turn them off right now." I thanked her again and went to get my keys. I could have sworn I turned them off when I got home, I thought as I got into the car. I decided that I was just distracted after my date—yes, that must be the answer. Then again, I couldn't help but wonder if this was another sign from Anna?

. . .

When I woke up the next day, I called Vicki to invite her over for dinner and see how everything was going with Mike. We sat at my kitchen table, waiting for some beef stew to warm up. I slid a glass towards her and started pouring some red wine.

"None for me please!" she said, darting the palm of her hand over the top of the wine glass.

"Since when do you say no to wine?" I asked, laughing.

"Well, that's part of the reason I wanted to see you, Ellen. I'm pregnant!" she squeaked, leaping out of her chair and jumping up and down excitedly.

"What? Wow! Was it planned?" I answered, half-smiling. I didn't know if I should be happy or worried for her.

"No! It's a complete surprise!" she yelped.

"Are you happy about it?" I asked, trying to gauge her reaction.

"I think so... I mean... yes, I guess I am."

She didn't sound too convincing.

"In that case, congratulations! When is the baby due?"

"The doctor said my due date is January second, but who knows, it could a Christmas baby!"

"I'm happy for you, Vicki. I really am."

I leaned in to hug her and noticed a big bruise on her right arm.

"What's this? What happened?"

"Oh, it's nothing. I must have hit my arm on the door frame. I do that all the time, I'm so clumsy!"

Were we really doing this dance again? This time, I decided to let it go. Babies change things, so they say, and I didn't want to upset my friend.

After dinner, we had tea in the living room and I told her all about Jack. She seemed genuinely happy for me.

"Do you think you'll see him again?" she asked, playfully teasing me.

"Maybe! I guess we'll just have to wait and see!" I answered back, trying to hide my genuine excitement. What I really wanted to talk to her about was the two people I saw in my bedroom a few days before, but I decided not to say anything because it would just worry her, and that was the last thing she needed right now.

"I should go. It's getting late," she said, snapping me out of my thoughts.

"Stay safe, Vicki, and please promise you'll call me if anything happens. You know you can come here anytime, right?"

"Don't worry about me, Ellen. I'll be fine."

We hugged goodbye, and I watched her get into her car and drive off.

How could I not worry about her?

. . .

The next morning, I sat at my desk working, on a new project that had just been assigned to me. Later, Linda informed me that she was moving to British Colombia because her husband had to help his father, who had fallen ill and could not manage the family business anymore. It saddened me to see her go, we had become such good friends.

"Where are you going in British Columbia?" I asked.

"Vancouver," Linda answered.

"Really, that's where Paul lives!" I hadn't thought about Paul in a while. I wondered what he was doing these days. "If you ever run into to him, say hello for me, okay?" I said jokingly, but secretly hoping she would.

When I got home from work, I had a message on my answering machine.

"Hey, Ellen, it's Jack. Listen, I know your birthday is coming up. Twenty-one is kind of a big deal, so I'd like to take you out to celebrate this Saturday. What do you say? Give me a call. Okay... well, bye for now." I stared at the machine. Maybe I should give him a chance. After all, there were more pros than cons, right? I called him back, but he didn't answer, so I left a message. "Hi, Jack. I'm returning your call. Saturday sounds good. Please call me back when you can and let me know when and where. Talk to you later. Oh... it's Ellen by the way." I put the phone down, feeling embarrassed—maybe he wouldn't call back and this would be the end of it. Just as I was about to give up hope, he called me back, and we agreed to meet at an Italian restaurant downtown.

• • •

On Saturday, I woke up refreshed and eager for date night. I let my hair down and put some makeup on, which I rarely did. I slipped into a red dress I bought especially for the occasion and wore my black high heels. I took a deep breath before leaving the house, and as I descended the front steps, I saw Donna sitting on the porch. "My, my, don't you look pretty tonight, Ellen! Going somewhere special?" she asked, getting up and twirling me around. "As a matter of fact, I am!" I said, blushing and feeling a bit more confident.

When I arrived at the restaurant, Jack was waiting for me outside. "Wow, you look amazing!" he said, his eyes lighting up. I returned the compliment, and then he put his arm around me and we walked inside together. The room was lit with dim candles and the sound of classical music created an air of romance. The hostess took us to our table and, when we sat down, Jack ordered a bottle of red wine. "Sorry, I should have asked what you'd like to drink. I hope you like wine," he said timidly. "Lucky for you, I do!" I answered, smiling at him flirtatiously. We sat for hours, staring at each other and enjoying the ambiance. After we finished eating, we ordered coffee and, just as I was ready to call it a night, he reached into his pocket and pulled out a small blue velvet box and said, "Happy twenty-first birthday, Ellen!"

"You didn't have to do that, Jack," I responded, hoping that he couldn't see my heart beating out of my chest.

"I know I didn't have to, but I wanted to. I hope you like it."

I opened the box slowly, my hands trembling. I let out a big sigh of relief when I saw that it was a gold chain with a heart pendant—I don't know what else I expected it to be.

"It's lovely, Jack. Thank you!"

He got up and stood behind my chair and put it around my neck, then leaned over to kiss me on the cheek. When he sat down, he took my hand from across the table, hesitated for a moment, and then asked if I would consider going steady. I didn't know what to say—was this good for me? Would I end up getting my heart broken again? I told him that I needed some time to think about it, which caused him to pull his hand away.

"Oh, well don't wait too long, Ellen. I'm a good catch you know!" he responded, making a joke to hide his disappointment.

I didn't know why, but the way he looked at me made me feel uncomfortable.

"If it's meant to be, it will be!" I assured him.

He winked at me, and we got up and walked to my car.

"So, Ellen, are you going to invite me over to your place for a night cap?"

"Not tonight, unfortunately. My parents might have people over, so maybe some other time," I lied. I wasn't ready to have him over to my place yet—I still wasn't sure about him and I didn't want to take the next step until I was.

"Don't take me for a fool. I know you don't live with your parents. Why would you lie to me?" he snapped, becoming defensive. I had never heard him speak this way before, and it caught me off-guard.

I felt my face turn red and struggled to come up with a plausible answer. Tension filled the air, until I finally muttered, "I'm sorry, Jack. I just wanted to get to know you better before getting too personal. I'm really tired tonight, so maybe another time?" Hopefully he would believe this, I thought.

"Don't worry about it, I get it. Another time then."

He leaned forward and, before I could turn my head away, he kissed me on the lips—I didn't hate it, but something still felt a bit off, so I quickly got in my car and left.

When I got home, I put the kettle on and changed my clothes before sitting on the balcony to drink some tea. An overwhelming scent of roses blew by. "Anna? If you're here, I need your help. Should I date Jack?" Suddenly, the coffee table started to vibrate and my cup went flying in the air before falling to the ground. "Oh shit, did you do that, Anna? This isn't funny!"

I got up, trembling, and opened the door to go inside. Then, everything went cold, and I heard a faint whisper, "Be careful, be very careful." I stood there for a few moments, contemplating what that meant, until Donna's voice filled the area.

"Are you okay up there, Ellen?" she shouted, stepping on the pieces of my shattered cup that had fallen onto her patio.

"Yes, I'm okay. Sorry about the broken cup, Donna, I dropped it by accident. I'll clean it up in the morning if that's okay?"

"No, don't worry about it. I got it. Goodnight, Ellen. Call if you need anything," she responded, looking slightly confused by the source of all this commotion.

Nothing made sense anymore. Who or what was Anna warning me about? I went back inside and laid down on my bed. It took me an hour to fall asleep, but soon after I did, I woke up to an unnerving feeling. I scanned the room, my eyes half opened. Out of the corner of my eye, I saw a dark figure standing at my bedroom door, silently watching me. I couldn't see its face, just its piercing red eyes. It began moving towards me like a dark cloud rolling in before a thunderstorm. I bolted upright as it extended its two hands, with long skinny fingers, out of its black robe. It grabbed me by the neck, tightening its grip, as I screamed Anna's name as loud as I could. I don't know how, but I found the strength to fight back—just like I did in the forest when I was twelve—and I pushed it off me before falling to the ground. The evil beast moved through the air and hit the night table, causing the lamp to fall and break, and it growled loudly before flying out of my bedroom.

I tried to catch my breath, shaking like a leaf and crying uncontrollably—what the hell was that thing? I mustered up the courage to check the apartment, cautiously entering each room in case it was waiting for me. When the coast seemed to be clear, I hobbled to the bathroom to get a glass of water and, as I looked at myself in the mirror, I saw two bright red marks around my neck. This was the proof I needed that I wasn't just imagining things. How could anyone deny my stories now? I stumbled back down the hallway, flicking on each light before reaching my room. I sat in the corner of my bedroom with my back against the wall—if it came back, I'd be ready.

• • •

In the morning, I called Vicki to tell her what happened. When she answered the phone, she sounded like she was crying.

"Vicki, it's Ellen. Are you okay?"

"Not really," she said, sniffling.

I told her to come over so we could talk, and then we hung up. When she arrived thirty minutes later, she looked weak and pale. She told me things had gotten worst with Mike, confessing that he'd kicked her in the stomach a couple of times, causing her to fall. She paused, tears flowing down her face, and then she told me that after this happened she noticed she was bleeding, so she went to the hospital. When she got there, the doctor tried to save the baby, but soon after, he informed her that the baby didn't have a heartbeat and she'd have to give birth to a stillborn.

"What kind of monster does that to the woman he supposedly loves?" she shrieked, shaking uncontrollably, heartbreak written all over her face. I held her in my arms and we cried together.

"How come you didn't call me, Vicki? I could have tried to help you get through this."

"I couldn't... Mike wouldn't let me. He told me that this is our business and no one else needs to know."

I begged her to leave him for her own safety, but she said that he apologized and promised that he would never hit her again. I didn't believe him, he had said this before. I insisted, but she was adamant about giving him another chance. I didn't understand or agree with her decision, but there was nothing I could do about it. Vicki was a grown woman and I couldn't force her to leave him if she didn't want to. I convinced her to stay overnight, so she called Mike and told him I wasn't feeling well and said she needed to take care of me. I'm sure he didn't believe her, but I didn't care. At least I could keep her safe for one night. After everything she had been through, I decided not to worry her by telling her about what happened to me the night before.

In the morning, we sat on the balcony to drink our coffee. "Look! There's a butterfly on your shoulder," she said, smiling. I got so used to the butterfly being around me that I hadn't noticed. Later, when she left, I made her promise to call me if she needed me, and I told her to call the police if Mike ever laid so much as a finger on her again.

I shouldn't have let her go.

CHAPTER NINE
RED ROSE

When I laid a pink rose on Anna's grave on the fourteenth anniversary of her death, I wondered what she would be like today, as a twenty-one-year-old woman. Would she be a veterinarian like she had always said she would? Would she be even more beautiful than she was as a young girl, with her long, golden locks? Even though it was short, I believed our friendship was one of the greatest gifts that life had graced me with, and I still missed her every single day. All of these thoughts and questions swirled around in my head as I sat on the soft grass beside her grave.

The next thing I knew, an hour had passed and, as I pulled myself up, a breeze swept through the cemetery, carrying a faint whisper, "Be careful, be very careful." I still didn't know what this warning meant and I wished that Anna would tell me more, or at least stop being so vague. I felt her presence and heard more whispers. At first, I couldn't make out what they were saying, but gradually it became clearer. "His eyes, look in his eyes," they said. "Tell me more, please!" I shouted back. I waited another ten minutes, but the air was silent, so I gave up and went back to my car, taking the butterfly with me on my shoulder.

That night, I drove to my parents' house for dinner, and when

I arrived, my mother opened the door, looking fragile and unwell. As soon as I entered, she began complaining about a sharp pain in her abdomen.

"Did you see a doctor?" I asked, worried and saddened that I couldn't do anything to help her.

"I've been putting it off, but I think I probably should," she answered, bent over in discomfort. "Anyway, never mind that. You're late, and dinner is getting cold."

The aroma from the roast beef resting on top of the oven made my stomach grumble. My mother slowly carried over two plates and placed them on the table in front of my father and me. "Here you go. If you don't mind, I think I'm going to lie down for a few minutes," she murmured, as she held her stomach. I glanced over at my father, but he didn't seem concerned. Something really had to be wrong if my mother was in so much pain that she didn't want to eat with us. My father and I ate quietly, making small talk here and there, and before I went home, I made my mother promise that she'd see a doctor. She finally agreed when my father jumped in and said he'd take her the following day. I kissed her goodbye, wondering if I should spend the night.

• • •

The next day, I couldn't concentrate at work. All I could think about was how much I regretted not taking my mother to the hospital the night before. I was anxious to hear my father's report about what the doctor said, so I tried calling him, but he didn't answer. When I got home from school a few hours later, I had a new message on my answering machine. "Ellen, it's Dad. You need to come to the hospital right away." The phone clicked. My heart sunk. I ran to my car and sped to the hospital. I must have been going too fast because bright blue and red lights illuminated the back of my car—I did not have time for this right now. I quickly pulled over and rolled down the window, shaking from fear and panic. A tall, good looking cop, perhaps in his mid-forties, casually walked up to my car. "Where are you going at that speed, young lady?" he inquired, before asking for my driver's licence. I reached over to get my purse, but it wasn't there—I left in such a hurry that it must still be on the table beside my answering machine. I begged him to let me go, trying to convey the urgency of my situation. "I'll bring my papers to the police station tomorrow morning, I promise! Please, my mother is in the hospital, it's an emergency. Please, can I go?" I pleaded, praying to God that he'd sympathize with my desperation. To my surprise, he let me off with a warning. I think he felt sorry for me.

When I finally rushed through the doors of the hospital, I saw my brothers and sisters sitting in the waiting room, crying and clinging to one another. My father was hidden in a room with my mother and we weren't allowed to go in and see her.

"Catherine, what is going on?" I demanded, my heart beating a hundred miles an hour, unsure whether I really wanted to know the answer. She put her arms around me. "Catherine, tell me now!" I repeated, this time louder and more forceful.

"Dad found Mom on the bathroom floor, unconscious. He called the ambulance, but she wasn't responsive when they took her in," she paused, knowing that what she was about to say would break me into pieces. "The doctors did everything they could, but she didn't make it. Mom's gone, Ellen."

I stood there for a few seconds, taking it in. This can't be real. I half expected Catherine to tell me she was joking and say that everything was fine, but why would she joke about something this awful. A wave of grief and guilt poured over me like nothing I had ever felt before, and tears started cascading down my face like a water fountain. Later, the doctor told us that she had a poisonous blood infection. From then on, I would always blame myself for not taking her to the hospital the night before. If I had, would she still be alive? When my father finally emerged from the room, he looked broken. "Your mother... she was a good woman," he cried. I had never seen my father cry before.

Later, we left the hospital and went to my parents' house. My father needed us—we needed each other. We sat in the kitchen and drank some tea, and, as I looked around the table, I realized how much time had passed since we had all been together, sitting in the kitchen as my mother prepared chicken soup—she always said it was good for us, masking the truth behind it. It seemed like such a long time ago, yet still so clear in my memory. Now, my brothers and sisters were all grown up. Daniel was off to college and Beth was in her last year of high school, while James and Catherine were living their own lives away from home. My father said that the house felt too big now that we were all rarely together under the same roof, but on that day, our mother's passing made us closer than ever, and we began to realize that we were all living on borrowed time.

I stayed for the night, and we reminisced about the good memories we had with my mother. The next morning, I woke up to the smell of bacon, so I eagerly went out to the kitchen, half expecting that my mother would be standing at the stove. If only this was all just a horrible dream. When I got to the kitchen, my father stood by the table, holding a plate of poorly-cooked eggs and bacon. "Your mother would have wanted me to do this," he stuttered, his puffy eyes revealed his pain.

"What's going to happen now, Daddy?" asked Beth.

"I'll have to get the funeral arrangements done in the next day or so," he said. Catherine volunteered to help—we couldn't let my father feel like he was alone.

• • •

The next day, I called Vicki to tell her the sad news. She cried with me on the phone. "Do you want me to come over, Ellen?" she asked. I told her that I'd be okay, I just needed to rest. As soon as I hung up, the shrill ring of the phone exploded throughout the room. "Ellen, it me, Jack. I've called four times since last night. Didn't you get my messages? Where have you been?" he asked, in an aggravated and off-putting tone. I told him about my mother and explained the suddenness of the situation, thinking that this would be an acceptable reason for not calling him back. He quickly said he was sorry and continued to emphasize his disappointment with me for not calling him the day before when he tried to get in touch. I had no words. How could someone be this insensitive?

"When's the funeral?" he pressed. "I want to go with you." I told him that this might not be appropriate—after all, he'd never met anyone in my family before. He insisted and wouldn't take no for an answer, saying that it was important for him to be there for me. I didn't have the energy to fight him on this, so I agreed and hung up, with Anna's warning ringing in my mind.

. . .

On the day of my mother's funeral, Jack met me at my apartment, and we took my car to the funeral home—I asked him if he wanted to drive, but for some reason he refused. Walking into the funeral home, I saw Vicki and her mother standing next to my father, who had his eyes fixated on the floor. I stood beside him and took his hand, he looked so fragile and pale. When I saw my mother lying in the casket, I reacted the same way I did when I saw Anna. This woman didn't look like my mother, her face was plastered with thick, clay-like makeup that made her look unnatural, especially considering she rarely wore any makeup when she was alive. I leaned closer to her, kissing her forehead, and whispered, "I love you, Mommy." I saw a tear under her right eye—it must have been one of mine. Or was it? I backed away from the casket, unable to take my eyes off her.

At the church, Jack and I sat in the front row. Midway through the mass, the minister called on me to deliver the eulogy. I walked slowly to the podium, my heart pounding, and asked my mother to give me strength to get through the reading without crumbling. I unfolded the parchment, which tied with a red ribbon. You could hear a pin drop in the church, the silence was so intimidating. I took a deep breath and read the words I had carefully written. At the end, my father joined me and shared some of his memories of my mother, barely able to contain his emotions long enough to speak. My brother came to the front, his guitar in hand. He played

"Let It Be" by The Beatles, accompanied by my dad at the piano. That was my mother's favourite song. The sound of people sobbing echoed throughout the melody.

At the cemetery, the minister read a small passage from the Bible before they lowered her casket into the ground, and, one by one, family and friends dropped a flower on top of it. "I hope you have a better life up there, Mommy. I hope the pain is gone. Goodbye, I love you," I whispered, as I let go of a long-stemmed red rose.

After everyone left, Jack and I walked over to Anna's grave. I couldn't stop crying, I was so mentally and emotionally drained. He held me so tight that I could feel his heart beating. "Maybe you shouldn't be alone tonight, Ellen. Let me stay with you." Again, I conceded—I couldn't resist his requests, it took too much energy— and I let him stay overnight, knowing it would change everything.

• • •

For the next few weeks, Jack and I grew closer and I finally let my guard down. He showed me he really cared about me—and he was nowhere near as bad a guy as Mike. Two months later, he asked me to marry him, and I said yes. I called Vicki right away to give her the good news, and she answered the phone with a meek, "Hello?"

"Vicki, guess what? I'm engaged!" Twisting the ring on my finger.

"What? To Jack?"

"Of course, silly. Who else would it be?" I laughed.

"Wow! I... well, let's just say I didn't expect this so soon. You sound happy!"

"I am, but it doesn't sound like you're happy for me."

I didn't understand her lack of enthusiasm, but I figured I must have caught her at a bad time. When I hung up, Jack went to the fridge to get a bottle of champagne that he had hidden behind a jug of milk. I thought it was presumptuous of him to have anticipated my response, but I needed the pick-me-up, so I accepted the glass. He suggested that we get married that summer, which felt a bit rushed, but I agreed. After all, who doesn't love a summer wedding? I asked him to move in with me while we looked for a bigger apartment, and the next day he showed up with just three bags filled with clothes and toiletries. I was looking forward to a new chapter and desperately hoped that everything would work out.

• • •

With the wedding fast approaching, it was time to shop for a dress, so Vicki and I made an appointment at a local bridal boutique. I had a tight budget, but I still managed to find the perfect dress. As soon as I tried it on, I instantly knew that it was the one. It fit me like a glove. "You look like an angel!" Vicki said, her eyes lighting up when I walked out of the changing room. "You're right! I am an angel," I giggled, feeling excited and happy.

When I got home, I prepared a nice dinner for Jack. I couldn't wait to tell him about my dress. "I'm so happy for you, princess," he said, hugging me.

"What about you? What will you wear?" He said he already reserved a black tuxedo. "We're all set then!" I said, counting down the days until we would be married.

When we went to bed, Jack fell asleep right away, even though the room was illuminated by a light I kept on so I could read. Lost in my book, I was startled when I felt a hand touching my hair. I turned to look over at Jack, but he was on his side facing the other direction. I turned back to inspect the other corners of the room, when I saw Anna standing next to the bed. I tried to contain my anxiety—and excitement—because I didn't want Jack to wake up. I had never shared that part of my life with him. He had no idea, and I wanted to keep it that way because he'd probably think I was crazy, like everyone else did. Anna looked at me straight in the eye and whispered, "His eyes. Look in his eyes," and then she disappeared. I was frustrated because all I wanted was to talk to her and find out more; it started to bother me, a lot!

I put my book down and turned off the light before leaning

over and putting my arms around Jack's waist. "Are you okay?" he moaned. "Yes. Go back to sleep, Jack," I muttered, as I dozed off.

• • •

After months of hard work, I received my paralegal certificate and accepted a new role at the law firm. "I'm so proud of you, princess," Jack said. He didn't graduate high school and never talked about wanting to do anything other than working in construction. I made more money than him, but it didn't bother me. We hunted for a two-bedroom apartment in our neighbourhood, and eventually we found one we both liked, not far from our current one. When it came time to sign the lease, Jack asked if I could do it on my own. I didn't understand why, but I couldn't argue about it with him in front of the landlord, so I signed the papers.

We went for dinner at our favourite Italian restaurant to celebrate, and sat at the same table as we did on our first date. After we were done eating, he handed me a gift box with a golden ribbon tied around it. To my surprise, it was another engagement ring, this time with diamonds and a large sapphire, which was my birthstone.

"It's beautiful, Jack! But why did you buy this for me?" I asked, puzzled. We needed to save our money now more than ever.

"This ring is much better than the other one, and you deserve nothing but the best, Ellen," he said. I wondered where he found the money to buy such an expensive ring, but I didn't bring it up.

We talked about our new place. "I'm confused," I started, treading carefully. "Why didn't you want to sign the lease with me today?" He barely let me finish before he hastily explained that he was recovering from bankruptcy and, although he had paid off his debts, his name wasn't cleared yet. I found this strange. Why didn't he bring this up before? A little voice inside me told me there might be more to it, but I ignored it. The last thing I wanted to do was start a fight, especially when we were out celebrating and the wedding was so close.

CHAPTER TEN
MESSAGES FROM THE DEAD

It seemed like perfect timing when a colleague at work recommended a psychic to me and gave me her number. I made an appointment for the next day, excited to finally get some answers. I pulled into the driveway and slowly walked up to the front door. I knocked lightly, and a tall, youthful woman opened the door. She looked nothing like a typical psychic, I thought, remembering Lucille from when I was younger. She had long, light brown hair and wore little makeup, and I was impressed with how sophisticated and trendy she was.

"You must be Ellen! Please, come in," she said, greeting me with a smile. I walked in, feeling more comfortable but still unsure about what to expect. "I'm Carmine. Follow me please," she said as we walked down the front hallway.

She took me down into to the basement and through a long corridor, where we reached a small room that was barely large enough for two chairs and a small table. "Please, have a seat and make yourself comfortable," she said, gesturing towards one of the chairs. She handed me a stack of tarot cards and placed candles around the room, carefully lighting each one, and she told me to hold the cards over my heart for a few minutes before shuffling them—seven times—with my left hand. I cut the cards in three piles and placed them on the table, from left to right. "Pick a pile," she said. I picked the middle one.

I had three questions:

1. Who was the woman with Anna?
2. What was it that I needed to be careful of?
3. What was behind the seventh door in my dream?

She laid the cards on the table in the form of a Celtic cross.

"Hmm, I sense that there is a lot going on in your life right now, Ellen," she said.

I knew that already.

"I see spirits around you... three of them."

"Three?" I asked. This surprised me. When I met Lucille a few years earlier, she told me that there were only two. Where did this other one come from?

"I see a little girl with long, golden hair. She's seven years old. Do you know who this is?"

"Yes, her name is Anna. She was my best friend, but she died when she was seven."

"She is with a woman with dark hair. Do you know who this woman is?"

"No. I think she has been around me for a while, but I don't know."

"I sense that she has been with Anna since the day she died."

This made no sense.

"Now, let's talk about the dark spirit," she continued, moving on, sensing my impatience.

"What dark spirit?"

"It's all around you. You need to be careful, Ellen," she warned.

"You're scaring me."

"Do you want me to stop?"

"No, please go on," I replied. I was terrified, but I needed answers.

"Ellen, your ability to communicate with the dead makes you vulnerable. You attract not only good spirits, but also bad ones. You need to make sure that you protect yourself."

"How can I do that?"

"Well, first you can cleanse your house by burning some sage in every room and opening all the windows to let the spirits out."

Next, she saw Jack in my cards, she described him to a tee.

"I see a wedding, but it won't happen. There's something—"

"Wait, what?" I interrupted. "Why? Is something going to happen to me... or to Jack?"

"I'm not sure, but something will get in the way of it. Something to do with your fiancé," she answered casually.

"Okay, now you're freaking me out. You're being too vague. If you can't be specific, I think I've heard enough," I snapped, growing more impatient.

"I can only tell you what I see in the cards, Ellen. I'm sorry if this upsets you. We can stop if you want, and you can come back some other time."

I quickly got up, paid her, and left. I didn't want to hear any more of this—it just angered me. How could she really know what the future held? Was she making this up to toy with my emotions? As I sped down the street, I felt a knot in the pit of my stomach. I stopped at the next corner, hesitant to go home—Jack would take one look at me and notice the fear and doubt in my eyes— so I sat on the side of the road for ten minutes, trying to calm myself down.

When I arrived home an hour later, Jack wasn't there, so I poured myself a glass of wine and called Vicki. I told her everything, except for my encounter with the dark spirit. She said that I should stop going to psychics because they just preyed on vulnerable people and came up with random predictions to confuse them.

"Everything will be fine, Ellen. You need to relax and ignore that crazy lady," she insisted. I kind of regretted telling her.

Jack came home later that evening, hobbling through the door, his eyes looking glassy.

"Where were you?" I asked, my heart pounding.

"Oh, I went for drinks with my guy friends after work."

"You could have called me to let me know. I was worried."

"Sorry, princess," he said, kissing me.

I looked at him in the eye and was overcome by a bad feeling.

"What's wrong?" he asked.

"Nothing," I said, moving towards the answering machine to check my messages before bed.

"Hi, Miss Taylor. This is Andy, your new landlord," the small black box blared. "I'm calling to let you know that everything is ready and you can pick up the keys anytime next week. Thank you." Click.

"That's exciting!" said Jack, "I'm really looking forward to moving into our new place!"

I wanted to be as excited as him, but I couldn't let myself be happy, still thinking about what Carmine had said earlier that day. I looked over at Jack as he reached for a glass of water and I noticed two deep scratches on his right arm.

"What's that? What happened to you?" I asked, moving towards him to get a closer look.

"Oh, that? It's nothing, I get scratches all the time. That's what happens when you work in construction!" he replied nervously, quickly covering his arm with his sleeve.

"Okay. I'm tired. I'm going to bed," I said, deciding not to press him.

"Wait a minute. You're not yourself, are you okay? Is something wrong?"

"It's been a long day, Jack. I just need to sleep."

I gave him a kiss on the cheek and walked to our bedroom to change my clothes. I heard him turn on the television and, later when he came to bed, I pretended to be asleep. I was lying on my side, facing the wall, and he rolled into bed and spooned me. "I love you," he whispered in my ear. I didn't get much sleep, my thoughts relentlessly dancing about in my mind.

• • •

In the morning, I kissed him on the cheek before leaving for work. "Hey, what's that all about?" he groaned. He grabbed me and kissed me on the mouth. "I'll see you at home tonight, doll," he said, smiling.

At the office, I went for coffee with Leah, the colleague who had recommended the psychic to me. When she asked me how it went, I wasn't sure how to answer.

"It depends how you look at it," I said.

"What do you mean?"

"Well, I think she was right about some things, but then –" I hesitated, I didn't want to get into the details. She knew better than to insist and instead asked how the wedding planning was going.

When we got back, I worked on a big case with my boss, which required a lot of research. He was pleased with the results and reiterated how lucky he felt to have me as his associate. "I'm telling you, Ellen, you'd make a great lawyer," he said. "Thank you, but that's not going to happen," I replied, laughing. I loved my job, but I had no intention of going back to school for a law degree.

When I got home, Jack was waiting for me at the door to give me a big hug. We ordered take-out and sat in front of the television to eat.

"Are you still excited about the wedding?" he asked, his mouth full.

"Why do you ask?"

"Well, you don't talk about it much these days."

"I am looking forward to it. I'm just tired and a bit low on energy lately, that's all," I assured him.

We snuggled on the sofa and watched an episode of "All in the Family," and I was just starting to fall asleep when I heard the doorbell. I pulled myself off the couch and went to see who it was.

"Hi, Donna, is everything okay?" I asked, opening the door.

"Yes, but I wondered if everything is okay with you?"

"Yes, why?" I answered, confused.

"Just curious because two policemen showed up earlier today. You guys weren't here so they knocked on my door and asked if I knew when you'd be home."

"The police? What did they want?"

"I don't know. That's why I thought I'd come by and check."

Jack heard us talking and came to the door.

"What's going on here?" he demanded, looking nervous.

"Donna said the police came looking for us today. Any idea why?"

"No idea. Why on earth would the police be looking for us?"

"I'm going to go now," Donna said, looking uncomfortable. I could tell she regretted coming over.

I closed the door behind her and stood in the front hallway, trying to find an explanation for their visit. I started to get worried that something might have happened to one of my siblings, so I called my father, but he said everything was fine.

"Jack, if you have any idea why the police were looking for us, you need to tell me now. I don't like surprises."

"Are you accusing me of something?" he said, getting defensive. I could see the rage simmering in his eyes.

"No, I'm just asking."

"I don't know, I promise you. Let's just go to bed and figure this out in the morning," he said, hoping that I'd drop it.

He put his arms around me and held me so tight it hurt, and then he led me to the bedroom. I didn't like this. Something was very wrong, and he felt like a different person.

"I love you so much. I won't let anything come between us, ever."

"Why do you say that?"

"I'm just telling you. Everything is going to be fine. Goodnight, princess," he said, getting into bed and turning off the light. He seemed different somehow, but I couldn't figure out why. I laid in bed for hours, unable to sleep, thinking that, just maybe, Carmine was right.

CHAPTER ELEVEN
WHAT DOESN'T KILL YOU

I couldn't stop thinking about all the times I heard Anna's ghost say, "Be careful, be very careful," but I still didn't understand what she was trying to warn me about. I had imagined so many scenarios, enough to drive me out of my mind, but nothing could have prepared me for what I was about to learn as I pulled into my driveway and saw a police car parked outside. My heart raced as I climbed the stairs two at a time. When I got upstairs, the door was slightly open, so I pushed on it and saw a police officer, with dark eyes and an angry expression, bolting handcuffs around Jack's wrists.

"What the hell is going on? Where are you taking him?" I shouted at the officer as I rushed towards Jack.

"I'm sorry... who are you?" asked his partner.

This feeling of panic and uncertainty transported me back to the day Anna was killed, the scene played on a loop in my head at a hundred miles an hour. I had to give myself a good shake to focus my mind and take in the present situation.

"I'm Ellen, Ellen Taylor, his fiancé. Why is he handcuffed?" I asked again, trying to stay calm.

"Your fiancé is under arrest, Miss Taylor," said the officer holding Jack.

"Arrested? For what?"

Jack couldn't look me in the eye, even when I tried to place my hand on his arm, and I could see guilt written all over his face. I began to worry about the seriousness of his arrest—did he hurt someone? Was it an accident? Was he wrongfully accused? All these questions swirled about in my head and I began to cry. I expected him to defend himself and explain what was going on, but he remained completely silent. The walls felt like they were closing in on me, and the anxiety I felt was immeasurable.

"We are going to take him to the station for questioning," declared the officer's partner.

"This is a mistake, right?" I pressed, looking at Jack and desperately trying to understand why this was happening.

He kept his head down, still ignoring my presence.

"Jack, ANSWER me!"

"Of course, it's a mistake! What do you think?" he snapped, his eyes looked hollow and his face emotionless. He was barely recognizable to me.

I asked the officers to give me a few minutes alone with him.

"Sorry, miss, but we have to go now. I'm afraid you'll also need to come with us."

"Why? Am I under arrest too?"

"No, but we do need to ask you a few questions."

I picked my purse up off the floor and followed them to the police car, where I saw Donna standing on her porch, looking deeply troubled—and even somewhat afraid. They helped Jack into the car, and I followed, sitting in the cramped, plastic-covered back seat. I felt trapped again when I realized that the rear door could not be unlocked from the inside. As we drove to the station, Jack still wouldn't look at me. Was it shame? Or did he not want to betray his guilt?

When we arrived, the officers ushered Jack to an interrogation room and took me to a separate room with a square table that had a recorder sitting in the middle of it. I stared at the blank white walls, thinking that they could use some colour, perhaps they were trying to intimidate me. A man dressed in a police uniform came in and closed the door behind him, I hadn't seen him before, but he seemed nicer than the men who arrested Jack. He was tall and thin, perhaps in his late thirties, and his eyes were hollow and red, which gave away the fact that he'd been up all night. As he stood in front of me, I scanned the equipment that dangled from his duty belt, and locked my eyes on his firearm.

"My name is Frank, I have a few questions and I'd like you to be precise and truthful with your answers."

Did he really think I wouldn't be?

"Please tell me what's going on," I begged. Why wasn't anybody telling me anything?

"Ellen, right?"

"Yes. Please tell me what's happening. I don't know what this is about," I asked again, growing impatient.

"What do you know about your fiancé's past, Ellen?"

I was about to respond, when I suddenly realized that I didn't have an answer because I barely knew anything about Jack's past. I felt embarrassed to admit it, so I stayed silent.

"Are you aware of his criminal record?"

"Of course not! What criminal record?" I answered, almost yelling. I thought maybe he had some unpaid driving fines, but I definitely wasn't prepared for what came next.

"Do you know where Jack was two nights ago, between five and nine?"

"He told me he went for drinks with friends after work. Why?"

"A fourteen-year-old girl was sexually assaulted that evening and we have reason to believe your fiancé was involved."

"What? NO! That's impossible! Jack could never do something like that!" I screeched.

I felt like someone was tearing my heart out, but I was still unwilling to believe that Jack was there that night. Frank slid a box of tissues across the table, and I realized that I was crying uncontrollably.

"Ellen, Jack did jail time for a similar crime before, so we know he's capable of this type of behaviour. We also have solid evidence of his involvement in the rape of that young girl."

"What evidence?"

"Like I said, I can't share all the details right now," he paused. I could tell he was hiding something.

I couldn't wrap my head around any of this. He continued talking, but I stopped listening, I couldn't take it anymore. My eyes moved to the corner of the room, where I saw Anna standing there looking at me, her eyes dimmed by melancholy. She pointed to her face, just above her left eye, and I could see a scar etched onto her skin—she was reminding me of Jack's scar. Then, a series of flashbacks raced through my head. I recalled the first time I saw Jack on the bus and how uncomfortable he made me feel, the way he looked at me, his eyes and the scar above his left eyebrow. My body turned as cold as ice, and I started to shake as I discovered why I had such a strange feeling around him.

Jack was one of the three boys who raped me in the forest when I was twelve.

"I think that's enough for today, Ellen. We can talk more tomorrow," Frank said, noticing the look of horror on my face as I made this discovery.

"What about Jack?" I asked, displaying my fear.

"We're keeping him in custody for now."

"How do I get home? I don't have my car."

"We can call a friend or family member to come pick you up."

He took me to the reception desk and handed me the phone. I called Vicki, and as soon as she answered, I started crying, unable to put two words together. "Calm down, Ellen. Just try to breathe. I'm on my way!" she said.

On the ride home, I told her everything, and she was just as shocked as I was. She offered to stay with me, and I couldn't refuse—there was no way I could be alone. As soon as we got back, I curled up on the couch, feeling disgusted and in disbelief that Jack had anything to do with the assault. I was upset with myself for not paying more attention to the red flags and listening to my gut feeling. My insides felt like they were on fire, burning ashes running through my veins.

"It's my fault, this is all my fault!" I wailed.

"Don't do that, Ellen, don't blame yourself. This is not your fault!" said Vicki.

"Fuck! I fell in love with my rapist, Vicki. What the hell is wrong with me?"

I went to the bathroom and threw up, then took a shower, got into my pyjamas, and pulled out the sofa bed for us to sleep on. I didn't want to be alone, and I certainly didn't want to sleep in the bed that Jack and I shared.

* * *

The next day, I went back to the police station and sat in the same interrogation room with Frank. I poured my heart out and told him everything that happened on that terrible day in the forest so many years ago. I couldn't prove it, but I was almost certain that Jack was one of the three boys—I could feel it in my heart, and the scar above his eyebrow was identical. I told Frank that my father reported the crime to the police at the time, but they never found them, and he assured me that they would reopen the case. Before we finished, he told me that Jack had been charged with theft and seven counts of sexual assault that took place over the last two years.

"Oh my God, how is that possible? He was always with me, he came home right after work every day, except for when he worked overtime."

"Ellen, Jack was fired seven months ago."

I couldn't believe what Frank was telling me, but when I really thought about it, everything began to come together—this explained why Jack didn't want his name on our lease and why I always ended up paying for everything all the time. I often wondered how he could afford the ring he gave me, and now I wondered if he had stolen it.

Frank pulled out a plastic bag from his pocket and put it on the table. My heart sank when I saw a gold chain with a pendent in the shape of a cross.

"Do you recognize this?"

"It's Jack's, I... I gave it to him for his birthday," I stuttered.
"How did you get it?"

"The girl who was assaulted had it in her hand when we found her, she must have torn it off Jack's neck."

I felt sick to my stomach, and covered my mouth with my hand. Frank opened the door and pointed me to the washroom across the hallway, before I ran to the toilet and vomited. I looked at myself in the mirror, my complexion pale as a ghost. Weak and shaky, I held on to the wall as I stumbled back to the room. Frank appeared, looking sincerely concerned for me, almost as a father looks at his daughter when she is lost and in need of guidance.

"We know it's him, Ellen, the evidence is undeniable."

"How... how is the girl doing?"

"She's in the hospital, she was badly hurt."

My heart exploded into a million pieces. I remembered the psychic saying that our wedding wouldn't happen—now more than ever I wish she would have told me why at the time. When I left the station, I drove home, feeling empty and completely hopeless, and I worried about what my family, friends, and colleagues would think of me. I lived with a monster, and even worse, I was going to marry my rapist. I wanted to disappear into that quiet place and finally let that dark spirit take me away.

•   •   •

When I arrived home, I ran up the stairs, trying to avoid Donna, but she followed behind me.

"Ellen, wait! I've been worried sick about you. Are you okay?" she asked, lightly pulling on my arm so that I would stop and talk to her.

I broke down, and she held me in her arms, just like a mother would.

"What is it, Ellen?"

"Something horrible has happened. Jack is going to prison!"

"Prison? Why?"

"He's a criminal, Donna... a horrible monster! I can't believe this is happening."

I told her everything, and she stared back at me with shock and disgust, covering her mouth with her hands in disbelief.

"Oh my God, Ellen, this is terrible! I would have never guessed this about Jack. He seemed like such a nice guy."

I went to the kitchen and made us a cup of tea, and we sat down at the table. I asked her if I could continue to stay in the apartment until I found a new place—I couldn't imagine moving into the one Jack and I had chosen together—and she told me that I could stay for as long as I wanted.

When she left, I took a long shower, hoping it would wash away the horrors of what I had discovered. I avoided our bedroom completely and made a bed on the sofa and turned the television on. As soon as I closed my eyes, I heard music, the kind that a ballerina box plays when you wind it up. I opened my eyes and saw Anna standing in front of me, tears surging down her cheeks. "What happened was not your fault, Ellen," she whispered, as her hand gently caressed my cheek. A sense of calm washed over me and we smiled at each other. I was about to ask her what I should do and if all of this was really true, when she vanished. I wondered why she never stayed longer.

• • •

The next morning, I called the office and told them that I needed to take a personal day—I couldn't face anyone, nor could I answer their questions about what was going on. I soaked in the bathtub for two hours in another attempt to scrub Jack off my skin. When I was done, I put on my jeans and a dark t-shirt and drove to the police station, where Frank had a cup of coffee on the table waiting for me.

"I wasn't sure what you take in your coffee," he said, dropping some sugar packets and creamers on the table.

"Thank you, that's very kind."

"Ellen, you said there were three boys who sexually harassed you. Do you remember what they looked like?"

"They didn't just sexually harass me, Frank, they raped me! I couldn't see their faces, it was dark and I was so blinded by fear."

"Go on," he nudged, trying to find any small piece of information that might be useful.

"I don't remember anything else. Oh my God Frank, do you think that Jack knew that it was me this whole time? Could he have targeted me?"

"We'll never know for sure, but anything is possible."

"I think you should check out Jack's two roommates. They lived with him before he moved in with me. I have a strange feeling that it could be them."

"Really… what makes you think that?" he said, his eyes rounded and eyebrows raised.

"My gut. You need to check them out right away. I think they all worked for the same construction company. Jack was always vague when I asked questions about them. It seemed like he didn't want me to get to know them."

After another long day of an endless string of questions, I went home and tried to get some rest. Something in me had changed. I no longer felt anything for Jack, I had no desire to protect him, I just wanted to find out the whole truth and make sure he got the punishment he deserved.

• • •

A few days later, Frank called me and asked if I could drop by, saying that he had more information to share. I got in my car and drove to the station, where I sat in the waiting room for thirty minutes, going through every detail to make sure I hadn't left anything out. When Frank finally walked in, he apologized for being late and said that he went to the hospital to talk to the girl's parents.

When we got to the interrogation room and sat down at the table, he informed me that they arrested one of Jack's roommates, saying that they had evidence that proved he was involved in other assaults in the area. I cried, speechless. Frank stood up and walked in a circle around the small room, gazing at the ceiling as if searching for the right words.

"What about the third guy?" I asked.

"We haven't found him yet, but don't worry, we won't stop looking until we do."

I felt like I'd never be safe again. After leaving the station, I drove to my father's house, and when I got there, he rushed over to me, hugging me tightly and saying that he had read about Jack in the newspaper.

"I tried to call you a million times, Ellen. Why didn't you call me back?"

"I'm sorry, Dad. I've been so busy dealing with the police and everything. I lost track of time."

"What a bastard, he deserves to die in jail!" he said, his face turning bright red.

I proceeded to reveal the details of Jack's sordid past and all the evidence against him that proved he was there that day in the forest.

"How could I not have known Jack was my rapist, Dad? I feel violated all over again," I cried as he held me in his arms.

"It was a long time ago, Ellen, please don't blame yourself," he pleaded. I could see that look in his face again, the one of regret because he wasn't there to protect me when I needed him the most. "They caught the bastard, that's what matters now. We finally have justice!" he said triumphantly, with his fist clenched in the air. I wondered what my mother would say if she were here, and in that moment, I missed her more than ever.

I stayed over at my parents' house that night and woke up feeling rested and hungry. As we sat together at the kitchen table eating breakfast in silence, I could tell that my family didn't know what to say, treading lightly so they wouldn't upset me. I finally spoke up and said that the wedding was cancelled, and Beth immediately came around the table and gave me a hug. "I know it's no consolation, Ellen, but it's a good thing you found this out before it was too late." I laughed hollowly and agreed, silently thinking about how close we were to getting married and that, if Jack hadn't been caught, I would have been his victim forever.

My thoughts were interrupted by a loud thump on the front porch before my father instinctually went to the door to retrieve the morning newspaper. When he came back into the kitchen, he looked puzzled, reading the front-page headline out loud. "Police Arrest Local Man, Karl Jackson, Accused of Sexually Assaulting a 14-Year-Old Girl." We looked at each other, confused, and he continued, "Police report that Jackson abducted the girl in the parking lot of a shopping mall, and that this allegedly was not the first time he preyed on young girls here. Jackson has been charged with seven counts of sexual assault, and police are still investigating other leads." Karl Jackson? Who was Karl Jackson? Did that mean Jack wasn't a criminal after all? What about the chain they found? I was certain that it was his.

I picked up the phone and called the police station, and they forwarded me to Frank. I blurted out my long list of questions, demanding to know if Jack would be released. Frank pleaded with me to slow down, and told me that they found out that Jack's real name was Karl Jackson, but they couldn't tell me until it was confirmed and approved to be released. I hung up the phone, feeling relieved but also infuriated—surely he could have told me before it was published in the newspapers.

My father paced the kitchen floor, panting. "Son of a bitch, I hope he gets what he deserves!" he shouted. I started crying as my adrenaline stabilized, and he wrapped his arms around me. "He's a monster, Ellen, a horrible monster." I decided to go home, I needed some time to think and, sooner or later, I'd have to face being alone in my apartment again.

Four weeks later, Karl was found guilty on all counts and sentenced to seven years in prison—this was far from enough, but at least it was something. I found out that the latest girl he attacked was still recuperating in the hospital. He should have been locked away for life for all the innocent souls he destroyed, I thought.

• • •

A few weeks after Karl was sent to prison, I picked up my mail and noticed an envelope from the correctional facility. My heart dropped—he wouldn't actually send me something, would he? I thought about throwing it in the garbage, but curiosity got the better of me, so I opened the letter, my hands trembling uncontrollably.

Dear Princess,

I hope this letter reached you. I think about you every minute of every day. You are the one person in my life who makes me feel alive. I can only imagine how you feel after all the lies they've said about me. You probably think I'm a monster, but I'm not. I have a big heart and I will love you until the day I die.

I'm sorry for the pain I caused you. I wish I could tell you this in person. I know you'll be all right, you're strong.

Please don't let this ruin the rest of your life, you deserve to be happy.

xoxo Jack

I stared blankly at the letter. I couldn't believe that he still referred to himself as Jack. This delusional and heartless bastard refuses to take responsibility for his actions, I thought as I paced angrily around the room. I debated whether I should reply to him, I even started writing everything I felt on the back of his letter: "I know who you are, Karl. You're nothing but a sick, pathetic monster. I hope you die in prison for your sins!" But then I took a deep breath, deciding that he wasn't worth it—as appropriate as my response would have been. He was right about one thing, though. I was strong. I picked up the letter, crumpled it into a ball, and burned it, determined now more than ever to move on and start a new chapter of my life.

CHAPTER TWELVE
ANGEL AT THE WHEEL

The next day, Vicki called and asked if she could come over. It was like she sensed that I desperately needed a friend. When she arrived at my apartment, she stormed through the door and shouted, "I have big news!" My first thought was that she was going to tell me that she and Mike were getting married. I held my breath for the news.

"Mike and I are officially separated!"

"What? Wow! Was it your decision?" I asked, trying not to express just how happy and relieved I really was.

"I guess you could say that. I couldn't take his endless abuse anymore. He nearly killed me last time."

"I'm so sorry, Vicki. I won't lie, I think it's the best decision you've ever made," I confessed.

"I have to move out," she said, tearing up, not from sadness, but from worry and uncertainty about the future.

"Move in with me," I answered, not hesitating for a minute. "We can look for a bigger place later!"

"You are the greatest friend in the whole wide world, Ellen! I knew I could count on you."

She moved all of her belongings in that weekend, and we

immediately started our search for a bigger apartment. We found a spacious two-bedroom in the same neighbourhood and moved in a month later.

* * *

I decided that it was time to go back to work and start getting back into my routine, and, after a couple of weeks, I finally started to feel like myself again. One Monday afternoon, as I sat at my desk sifting through a project I was working on, my phone rang, and, when I answered it, Linda was on the other end. I hadn't heard from her since she moved to Vancouver. She told me that she ran into Paul at a technology conference the week before, explaining that he was a speaker on one of the panels she attended. She figured it was him, remembering the description I had given her, and said that she went to his company booth after lunch and introduced herself. When she mentioned my name, his face turned red and he invited her out for coffee. After thirty minutes of casual conversation, he finally asked how I was doing and, before they parted ways, he gave her his business card and told her to give me his number. I asked her if he mentioned a girlfriend or wife, but she said he didn't, before adding that he wasn't wearing a ring either. I wrote his number on a piece of paper and put it in my purse. I couldn't stop thinking about it all day and, as soon as I got home, I told Vicki, but she said that she didn't think calling him would be a good idea.

"It took you an eternity to get over him, Ellen. Why would you want to reopen old wounds?"

"What do you mean reopen old wounds? My wounds never healed, Vicki," I snapped back, getting defensive. "Paul is one of the only decent men I have ever met, and he was nothing but kind to me. How could I not call him?"

She made me doubt myself, though, so I took the piece of paper from my purse and threw it in the garbage, unwilling to trust myself ever again when it came to choosing men.

* * *

On my twenty-second birthday, Vicki and I went to the same pub we always went to—it was becoming a fun tradition that we both looked forward to every year. We were listening to the band, when Vicki suddenly elbowed me in the side and whispered, "I think the guy at the next table is checking you out!" A few minutes later, I turned to look at him, and we smiled at each other, then he got up and joined us at our table. As we started talking, we realized that we went to high school together; I was embarrassed because I forgot his name. "Derek," he said. We spent the next hour talking about all the people we used to know, wondering what they were all doing now. He asked if I was still in touch with Paul, and I told him that my friend gave me his number, but I didn't call him.

"What are you waiting for?" he asked.

"I'm not sure if it's a good idea. He did break my heart, you know."

"I think you should call him," he insisted, looking mysterious. "It might be a good idea for you two to talk."

I was confused. Why was he pushing me to call him?

• • •

A couple of days later, I still couldn't stop thinking about Paul, so I decided to clear my head and go to the cemetery to visit Anna. It was a calm and sunny morning, and I could hear the wind rustling the leaves of nearby trees. I looked around and couldn't see anyone, but I felt surrounded by so many souls. I heard murmurs, as though they were having a conversation with each other. I went to my mother's grave first and it saddened me to see my father's name engraved below hers without a deceased date. What a peculiar ritual, I thought.

I walked over to Anna's grave and sat down to talk to her, asking if heaven was better than earth and if our mothers were together. I also told her that, even though I wanted to see her now and then, she shouldn't appear to me out of nowhere in the middle of the night because it frightened me. I wondered what people might think if they heard me talking to a tombstone, but to me it almost felt like a normal thing to do. A butterfly landed on my shoulder and two others floated around me. This was reassuring, and I took it as a sign that Anna was listening to me—and maybe even our mothers too. I looked up to the sky and blew kisses to them, and when I walked back to my car, the butterflies followed me, just like they always did.

• • •

Time flew by so quickly, and the next thing I knew, there were only seven more days until Christmas. I got up and looked outside, marveling at the snowflakes falling slowly through the silent air, dancing to the ground. After breakfast, Vicki and I decided to brave the mall to do some Christmas shopping.

Three hours later, we arrived back home and dragged our shopping bags up the stairs to the third floor of our building. As soon as we got in, we emptied them onto the living room floor and wrapped our gifts, while our famous Christmas cookies baked in the oven. As we were finishing up, we heard a knock on the door, and when I opened it, our next-door neighbour stood outside. He was an attractive man, younger than most of the other people in our building, with blonde hair and piercing blue eyes. He reminded me of James Dean, one of my favourite actors. I had seen him around the building once or twice, but had never spoken to him. He asked if he could use our phone, saying that his wasn't connected and he needed to make an important call. He took out a long-distance phone card and started dialing numbers on the keypad.

"Hi, can you connect me to room three-seven-seven please?" he asked.

"Hi, Mom, it's Robert, how are you?" he paused, listening intently. "I'm so sorry to hear that, are you in a lot of pain? What did the doctor say today?"

It didn't sound like good news.

"Okay, hang in there. I'll be there tomorrow. I love you, Mom."

"Robert, right?" I asked, as he hung up the phone.

"Yes, sorry I should have introduced myself. What's your name?"

"Ellen, and this is my best friend and roommate, Vicki."

His eyes locked onto Vicki's and he blushed.

"Thank you for letting me use your phone. The phone company was supposed to install mine yesterday, but the technician never showed up."

"No problem at all. Is your mother okay?" I asked.

"Ellen, maybe Robert prefers not to talk about this personal matter," Vicki said, nudging me with her elbow.

"It's okay. She's in the hospital… she has stage four cancer."

"Oh no, I'm so sorry," I said, covering my mouth with my hand.

"You shouldn't be alone at a time like this," Vicki said, lightly grazing his right arm.

"Would you like to join us for dinner?" I asked, trying to break the tension.

He looked hesitant, but said yes. We sat down at our kitchen table, and I opened a bottle of wine and turned on the radio. He stayed for about an hour, and we got to know him better. He was easy to talk to and seemed different than the other men we knew. The attraction between him and Vicki was palpable, and I started to feel like a third wheel, though I enjoyed watching them flirting with each other. Vicki looked saddened when he got up to leave, saying that he had a two-hour drive the next day to see his mother.

"Good luck. If you need anything, anything at all, don't be shy," I said.

"Thank you again. You're both very kind," he smiled back, locking eyes with Vicki one last time before he left.

• • •

On Christmas morning, I woke up feeling my mother's presence. I knew when she was around, I could smell her Player's cigarette burning. I found it strange that this was her way of letting me know she was around me because she knew how much I hated that smell. I couldn't see her, but her presence made me feel safe and protected.

I got up and went to the living room, still in my pyjamas, and made some coffee. Vicki came into the kitchen a few minutes later and we opened our gifts together. I let her open hers first, smiling as she unwrapped it slowly, making sure she didn't rip the paper so she could use it again, she always did that. She looked surprised and overjoyed when she saw the Canon camera I bought for her. A few weeks ago, we booked an all-inclusive trip to Mexico together, and she was excited that she'd be able to capture all our memories there. She immediately took a few pictures of me—I never liked having my picture taken. "Get used to it, girl, I'll be taking a bunch when we get to Mexico!" she said excitedly. She handed me my gift, a pretty yellow dress with a pink trim, perfect for our trip.

• • •

Vicki invited me for Christmas dinner at her mother's house, and I told her I'd meet her there later, after I had lunch with my own family. The snow continued to fall, and when I left my father's house later that afternoon, the roads were slippery and the visibility was poor. I slowly followed the car in front of me for about ten minutes, until the driver unexpectedly slammed on the brakes, when he noticed a police car parked on the opposite side of the road. I also hit my brakes, causing my car to spin out of control, turning one hundred and eighty degrees directly towards the police cruiser. It all happened so fast, and I didn't have time to react. In a fraction of a second, my car came to a full stop, parallel to the police car, missing it by an inch. The officer got out of his car from the passenger side, and I rolled down my window.

"Are you okay?" he asked, looking rattled.

"I think so," I said, still trying to catch my breath.

"I've never seen anything like this in my life. How did you manage to stop your car dead in its tracks?"

"I don't know, it's a miracle I guess."

A whiff of cigarette smoke manifested, and I knew that my mother saved my life. She had her hands on the wheel, I was convinced of it.

"An angel must have saved us," I said.

"I believe you, young lady. I can't think of any other explanation."

He asked for my driver's license and insurance papers, took a quick look at them, and gave them back to me. "We were both very lucky today, Miss Taylor. Drive safely," he said as he walked back to his car.

All I wanted to do was go home, and when I got there, I went to bed, feeling full of love and happiness knowing that my mother was there with me on Christmas.

• • •

I still had a couple of boxes to unpack from our move, so I decided to tackle the project one rainy day after work. When I opened the last box, I found my Ouija board tucked away at the bottom, looking neglected yet perpetually ominous. I pulled it out slowly and placed it on the kitchen table, staring at it and remembering its warning about Zozo so many years ago. Caught up in my thoughts, I failed to notice Vicki's arrival.

"What the hell, Ellen? I thought you got rid of that stupid thing!" she shrieked, ripping it off the table. "You shouldn't keep it in the apartment! Don't you remember what happened last time we played? It's bad luck to have it here!"

"I can't get rid of it yet, I still need answers," I replied bluntly, transfixed by the board.

"Answers to what?"

"So many things, like what's behind the seventh door I keep seeing in my dream."

"You're obsessed, Ellen, but if you want to try it out again, I guess I'm in."

I was somewhat surprised by her response, but all the more eager to see what the board would reveal. She closed the blinds, and I lit some candles, and we sat on the living room floor, crossing our legs and putting the board on our knees. With our fingers placed carefully on the planchette, I began asking questions.

"Spirit, are you here?"

The pointer slowly moved to *YES*.

"Jesus! Did you do that, Ellen? Now I remember why I don't like this game!" Vicki yelped.

I ignored her and continued. "Spirit, is there someone behind the seventh door in my dream?"

The pointer moved slightly and then veered to *YES* again.

"Spirit, is this person alive?"

Nothing happened for a moment, and then it moved to *NO*.

"Spirit, is it a woman?"

It slowly moved to *YES*.

"Spirit, do I know this woman?"

The pointer began moving rapidly around the board, pointing to the letters, spelling out *NOT YET*.

"Okay, Ellen, that's enough. I'm scared! I don't want to do this anymore!"

I pulled my fingers away from the pointer, this was enough information for now, and then quickly moved it to *GOODBYE* before folding the board and putting it back in its box.

"Thank you for doing this with me, Vicki, I know how much you hate it."

"I've said it before and I'll say it again, Ellen, I don't think you should keep this board. I don't have a good feeling about this."

I got up and took it to my bedroom to hide it in the back of my closet. When I returned to the kitchen, I made us tea, as Vicki sat completely still and quiet.

"At least now I know there's something behind the seventh door, but I wish I knew the identity of the woman and the boy."

"I don't think you'll find your answers by asking Ouija, Ellen. Just leave it alone."

We slept in the same room that night, Vicki was too scared to be alone.

• • •

Our trip to Mexico was coming up, and with only two weeks left, we started packing our bags. As we folded our clothes and placed them in our suitcases, Vicki started talking about Robert—over the last few weeks, she brought him up more often—and said that she wondered what he had been doing lately.

"You totally have crush on him, don't you?" I teased.

"Well, he's nice and he's cute, don't you think?" she answered, blushing.

We hadn't heard from him since he had dinner at our place, so we decided to knock on his door. When he answered, he looked somewhat surprised to see us, and told us that his mom had passed away the week before. After we offered him our condolences, Vicki asked him to join us for a drink at our place. When we got back, I opened three beers, and we sat in the living room. He described how his mother suffered to the very end, giving vivid and painful details. Seeing him cry broke my heart, I could tell he was extremely fond of her and that he admired her. He told us that she was a psychologist and devoted her life to assisting those in need, and then he began a long story about her helping a young boy to cope with the loss of his mother, who had passed away when he was only seven years old. I had chills all over my body—I couldn't help but think about the boy in my dream.

"Would you like another beer?" Vicki asked.

"No, I'm good. I should probably go," he replied, looking worn down and upset.

When he got to the door, he noticed our luggage in the living room.

"Going somewhere?"

"Yes, to Mexico! Maybe we'll get to see you before we leave?" Vicki asked.

"Maybe," he said, winking at her before he left.

I went to bed with a strange feeling that our paths must have crossed for a specific reason. As I rested and read a book, my body started to vibrate and then went into a state of complete paralysis. Having experienced this before, I knew exactly what was happening to me. I floated above my body and went flying into a long and narrow tunnel, until I stopped and saw seven people around a table. Anna was sitting beside a woman, and this time I could see her face, but I didn't know who she was. She looked at me and smiled, and while I could see her lips moving, there was no sound. I felt something pushing me further into the tunnel, and then it became dark and I was completely blind. I tried to turn back, but remained pinned in place until, out of nowhere, I felt something grab my legs, trying to pull me in further. I tried to scream, but nothing came out. Suddenly, I felt my hands grabbing a rope, which swung me back into the white tunnel and abruptly hurled me back into my body. It took five minutes before I could move again, and I slowly got out of bed, drenched in sweat and my head spinning.

Whatever was going on with me, I didn't like it.

CHAPTER THIRTEEN
SHADOWS OF REALITY

"Finally! We're going to Mexico tomorrow!" Vicki shouted, dancing around my room in excitement. "What's going on?" she asked, noticing that I didn't seem as enthusiastic. I told her I was fine, but I didn't want to admit that I was afraid of flying. I knew that everything would be okay, but the thought of floating through the air with absolutely no control frightened me. We finished packing our bags and ate a light dinner before we went to bed early to catch our flight the next morning.

When we woke up at 4:00am, I started getting excited by the prospect of escaping my routine for a week. The flight was uneventful—I even enjoyed it, largely due to Vicki's enthusiasm and good humour. When we arrived in Cancun, we changed into our shorts and t-shirts and went to sit on a patio, gulping down a couple of Coronas. We scanned through the pamphlets they gave us at the reception desk, and booked a tour of Tulum for that Wednesday.

After a while, the heat and alcohol started making me tired. "Let's go for a walk along the beach, it'll wake us up," Vicki suggested, pulling me up off my chair. On our way, we saw a group of guys basking in the sun. They whistled at us, and I wanted to run, but Vicki seemed to be amused. "Come on, Ellen, loosen up, they're cute! A little flirting never hurt anybody!" One of them got up and introduced himself. "Hi, I'm Harry," he said, extending his right hand. He was tall and handsome, with blonde curly hair, beautiful milk chocolate eyes, and dark, tanned skin. His friend followed him. "This is my friend, Ray," Harry said, both of them smiling at us. We chatted with them for a while, and then Harry invited us to a party they were having on the beach later that night. "Sounds like fun," Vicki said, telling them that we'd be there. I elbowed her, and she smirked. "We're here to have fun, Ellen, remember?" she whispered, as Harry and Ray looked at us expectedly. Vicki was always much more spontaneous than I was, but maybe it was time for me to loosen up and try to have some fun.

We continued walking along the shore line, and I was mesmerized by the beautiful rays of reds and yellows bursting from the sun. "Your freckles are in full bloom!" Vicki said as she touched the tip of my nose. I frowned, I hated my freckles. "Stop it, you look adorable!" she said. I remembered how Anna and I always used to compare our freckles and try to count them, but then we'd quickly give up because there were just too many.

We went back to the hotel to freshen up and put on our favorite summer dresses for dinner. On our way out, we bumped into Harry and Ray. "Fancy running into you ladies. Are you joining us for the party tonight?" Harry said. "Sure, we'll be there after we have dinner," Vicki replied. "Why don't you eat with us, we're having a barbecue on the beach." Vicki looked at me for approval, so I nodded. "Follow us," Ray said, impressed with himself.

After we ate, we sat around a bonfire and Harry played the guitar. "Hey, Ellen plays guitar too!" Vicki shouted, nudging me to join in. I gave her a stern look and said that I didn't want to play— I didn't want to embarrass myself in front of so many strangers. Harry ignored my trepidation and handed me his guitar. "Come on, I dare you!" he urged. I took the guitar and played a song by The Beatles, and they all sang along. I ended up having fun, smiling and gaining confidence as I moved on to another song.

I was always amazed at how the world can be so big and yet so small. As I talked to Harry more, we found out that we were from the same place back home, just a few blocks away from one another. What were the chances that I would meet someone from my neighbourhood, in Mexico of all places! I started to like him, he reminded me of Paul. At the end of the night, he gave me his phone number. "Call me some day. I have a gig at the North Pub, I play music there every Friday and Saturday night. You could join me on stage sometime, if you feel like it." Just the thought of getting on stage gave me anxiety. "I'm way too shy for that!" I said, feeling my face turn red.

After a couple of days relaxing on the beach, we developed a close friendship with Harry and Ray. On Wednesday, they joined us on a guided tour to Tulum, where we saw the ruins of Chichen Itza. The history of the Maya fascinated me, especially because the tour guide said that people had seen ghosts wandering through the pyramids and other ruins of the city. I felt surrounded by these spirits and, as we explored the site, I heard faint whispers that were inaudible to everyone else. In a strange way, I was at home, unlike Vicki who couldn't wait for it to be over.

• • •

That year, I turned twenty-four and, on my birthday, Vicki and Robert, who had become a couple, invited me over for dinner at his place. When we were almost done eating, Vicki announced that she and Robert planned on moving in together. This news made me sad, but I was comforted by the fact that he lived in the same building, so I could still see her as often as I wanted. After dinner, Vicki handed me a small, wrapped box that contained tarot cards. "I got these for you because I think they're a bit safer than Ouija," she said, winking at me.

• • •

Later, as I laid in bed, I couldn't get Harry out of my mind. I thought about his proposition to perform with him onstage, but then my thoughts quickly shifted to Paul. I felt the urge to talk to him, and I regretted throwing out the paper with his number on it. I called Linda the next day, and luckily she still had his business card and was able to give me his phone number and address. That night, I decided to write him a letter.

Dear Paul,

I hope this letter reaches you and that you have been doing well. It's been a long time. My friend Linda said she met you at a conference and she gave me your information. I know you saw her a while ago, but I didn't have the courage to reach out to you until now. I think about you often, I never really got over you. You were my first love. I still wonder what happened and why you stopped calling me.

If you would like to get in touch, my address is listed on the front of the envelope. I would love to hear from you.

Love always,

Ellen

• • •

The next morning, I mailed the letter on my way to work, but the minute I dropped it in the mailbox, I regretted it. Coincidently, Linda called me at the office that day and reported that she had read in the paper that Paul had been appointed to the role of Director of Research and Development for a large technology company. I told her that I mailed him a letter that morning to the address she had given me, which I assumed was his old business address. I wondered if he would still receive it, but maybe it was better if he didn't, I concluded.

"Why didn't you call him instead of writing him, Ellen? I really think you two need to talk."

"I'll wait to see if he responds to my letter. Maybe the people at his previous company will forward it to his new address."

That evening, I pulled out my tarot cards. I read the instructions and lit a few candles before placing the deck over my heart, focusing on my questions. I shuffled the cards seven times with my left hand, and then split the deck into three piles. Then, I took the middle pile and spread the top ten cards on the table in the shape of a Celtic cross. For the most part, my interpretations of the cards were validated by the descriptions in the book. I was disturbed by the Death card, placed over the Devil card, which was represented by a naked man and woman chained to a pedestal on which the Devil sat. It gave an eerie feeling and left me with more questions than answers. Too afraid to find out more, I put the deck back in the box and went to bed.

· · ·

Later that week, my boss asked me to work overtime to help him complete a report he needed for the following morning, so I had to stay late at the office. It was pitch black by the time I got into my car, and I decided to take a different route so I could stop at McDonald's. I wasn't hungry, but something pulled me in. I ordered a hot chocolate and, as I walked out of the building, I saw a frail old lady struggling to get the door open as she clung on to her walker. I went over to help, opening the door for her.

"Can I help you with something, ma'am?" I asked.

"No, thank you, but I'll walk out with you."

I figured she was confused, so I walked with her.

"Is someone waiting for you in the parking lot?" I asked, wondering where she was going.

"No, I have to go home."

"Where is home?"

"On Harvest Street."

I used to live on that street. There's no way she could walk that far, she could barely put one foot in front of the other, and it was way too late for her to be walking alone.

"Can I give you a ride home?"

"That would be nice, dear, thank you."

I held her arm and we walked slowly to my car. I helped her get in the passenger's seat and then I put her walker in my trunk. When we arrived on Harvest Street, I asked her for the house number.

"Right there," she said, pointing to a brown apartment building on the left.

"What a coincidence, I used to live in that building!"

"I know, dear," she said looking at me straight in my eyes.

I couldn't remember seeing her in my building before, but thought that perhaps she had seen me around at some point. I parked the car and helped her get out of her seat, and she began to walk, without her walker, which seemed odd because she wasn't able to take a step without it just minutes before. I held her arm and walked with her inside the building before offering to accompany her to her apartment. When I asked her what floor she lived on, she stared at me blankly, then said, "Seven."

"I used to live on that floor as well! What a coincidence!"

"Yes, I know, dear."

I asked her how she knew that, but she didn't respond. When we got out of the elevator on the seventh floor, she walked down the hallway and, taking out her keys from her purse, she stopped at the last door on the left side—this was the exact apartment I used to live in!

"Here, open it, dear," she said, giving me the key.

I opened the door and couldn't believe my eyes. The interior was an exact replica from when I lived there with Vicki—everything from the furniture and decorations, to the picture frames and flower vases. It felt like I was in a twilight zone, and then she took my arm with her ice-cold hand.

"Please come in, I have something for you," she said, grabbing the brown bag that sat on the entrance table. "What is this?" I asked, taking it from her. She looked at me with her stern eyes, "Just take it, but don't open it until you get home," she demanded. I left, leaving the door open behind me. When I got into my car, I realized that her walker was still in my trunk, so I took it out and went back to her apartment. Her front door was closed and locked, and she didn't answer when I knocked, so I left it outside.

When I got home, I soaked in a hot bath for an hour, thinking about what happened that night. None of it made sense. I put on my pyjamas, poured myself a glass of wine, and sat on the sofa, staring at the brown bag that rested on my lap. It took me fifteen minutes before I got up the nerve to look inside. I carefully opened the top, making sure I didn't rip it. It felt light, but I could tell something was sitting at the bottom, so I reached in and pulled out a golden lock of hair that was tied with a blue ribbon. It looked just like Anna's, I had to pinch myself to make sure I wasn't dreaming. I went from feeling intrigued to petrified. Who was this old lady? This wasn't the first time that I didn't have an explanation for finding Anna's hair. I placed it in a box with the others and went to bed, leaving the lights on.

• • •

I visited the cemetery that weekend, and on my way home, I stopped at the old lady's apartment to make sure she found her walker. I thought this would also be a good opportunity to ask her more questions, but when I buzzed her apartment from the lobby of the building, she didn't answer. A man happened to walk in at the same time and he let me in, and we took the elevator together. When he got off on the seventh floor, I walked behind him and saw him unlock the door of the old lady's apartment. As he was about to go in, he saw me standing behind him and asked who I was looking for. I stared at the inside of the place, speechless, the furniture and décor were completely different. He looked at me, his dark black eyes piercing right through mine.

"Um… hello? How can I help you?" he asked again.

"Do you live here?"

"Well, let's see, I have the key and I unlocked the door, so what does that tell you?"

"I'm sorry, I'm just confused because—"

"It's okay. You seem a bit lost. Who are you looking for?"

"Is there an old lady who lives here?"

"An old lady? No, I'm afraid not. You must have the wrong apartment number."

"I'm really sorry… it's a long story, but I helped an old lady to this apartment just a couple of days ago. She had the key and I opened the door."

He gave me a strange look, not knowing whether I was confused or completely crazy. "That's not possible. I've been living here for a couple of years now. Maybe she's on a different floor and you mixed them up."

"No, I'm sure it was here, but the place looks different today, which is strange."

"Hey, you look like you could use someone to talk to. Would you like to come in?" he asked. I wouldn't usually go in a stranger's place, but he was right, I did need someone to talk to. "I'm Gary by the way. And you are?" he asked, holding the door wide open.

"Ellen Taylor," I answered.

"Nice to meet you, Ellen. Please come in, I'll make us some coffee."

He took me to the kitchen and told me to sit down at a small rectangular table that was nestled into the corner by the door. My eyes wandered to the floor, which had deep scratches that I made when I lived there. Gary placed two mugs on the table and sat down beside me.

"Talk to me. What's going on?" he asked, taking a sip of his coffee.

When I told him about my bizarre encounter with the old lady, he seemed intrigued.

"Had you ever seen this woman before that night?"

"No, and I left her walker at the door. Did you see it?"

"Actually, I did, but I didn't know whose it was, so I took it to the superintendent's office."

"Did anyone claim it?"

"No. I've lived here for two years and have never seen the old lady you described."

"But she had a key to this apartment!"

"Right. But it's not possible, Ellen. I'm the only one who has a key."

This didn't make any sense, I was so frustrated and confused. I took one more sip of my coffee and told him I had to leave. "I realize we just met, Ellen, but please know that I'm here if you need to talk. I'm a good listener." He seemed sincere, I felt at ease with him. He gave me his business card and I slid it into the side pocket of my purse.

. . .

When I got home, I bumped into Vicki in the hallway as she was going out. "Hey! Are you okay? You look pale," she said. "I'm okay, I think." She looked at me and frowned. "I can tell something is wrong, but if you don't want to talk about it that's fine. Just know that I'm here whenever you're ready." Before she left, she added that Robert was out for the evening and she was having a few friends over. She told me to come, and I agreed—I could use the distraction. I went to my place to freshen up and get changed, and grabbed a bottle of wine before going to Vicki's. I appreciated the company and great conversations with plenty of laughs, it took my mind off things.

"Girls, I have big news! Robert and I got engaged yesterday!" Vicki announced, standing up and showing off a diamond ring that adorned her finger.

"Wow! Congratulations! When's the wedding?" I asked, a bit hurt she didn't tell me first.

"We haven't set a date yet, but we are thinking sometime in the fall."

The rest of the evening revolved around discussing Vicki's wedding plans. When her friends left, I stayed with her for another hour, and told her all about the old lady and Gary.

"Wow, slow down, Ellen. This is a lot to take in. How is any of this even possible?" she asked.

"I don't know, Vicki. I'm starting to think there's something seriously wrong with me."

"Maybe it's time for you to get some professional help. Is it possible your mind is playing tricks on you?"

"Are you saying I'm making this up?"

"No! I'm just saying it might help to talk to someone other than me, that's all."

"You think I'm crazy."

"Oh, Ellen. No, I don't. I'm just trying to help. I don't know what else to say."

She suggested that I sleep over at her place that night. "Don't be silly, I live right next door," I said, giving her a hug. When I got back to my apartment, I shut off all the lights and went to my bedroom. As soon as I hopped into bed, the room turned cold and I heard a faint whisper, "Be careful Ellen, be very careful." I couldn't see Anna, but I knew it was her voice. The last time she told me to be careful was before Jack was arrested, and this gave me a terrible feeling that something bad was about to happen to me again.

CHAPTER FOURTEEN
CLOSURE

It was that time of year again, when autumn quickly ushers in the sharp coldness of winter. I always felt short-changed when winter snuck in like a burglar, wrapping everything in a shimmery white blanket. I could almost hear it whistling—"Look at me, I am the king of the seasons!"—before Christmas came waltzing in, accompanied by an array of emotions. I missed my mother, I didn't always understand why she acted the way she did when I was younger, but now I was starting to. I learned that she struggled with untreated depression for years, which explained a lot in retrospect. I loved her, and as she got older, she became less hesitant to tell me that she loved me too.

. . .

When I woke up on Christmas morning, I turned on the radio and listened to some carols to put me in the right mood for the day. Later, I went to my father's house for dinner, and the delicious scent of roasted turkey and ragout floating in the air made me hungry— this was definitely the best part of Christmas! In the evening, as tradition would have it, we all sat in front of the fireplace, drinking eggnog while my siblings listened to my brother and I play the guitar. When I told James that Harry suggested that I come play with him at the local pub, he quickly became my biggest cheerleader and encouraged me to take him up on his offer. I admired my brother for his musical talent and, like my father, he was a natural, but I wasn't convinced I was good enough to get onstage in front of all those people. Maybe it was time for a New Year's resolution.

When I got home later that night, I dug through my bag, looking for the paper Harry wrote his number on, and instead found the business card that Gary had given me before I left his apartment. I was surprised by the inscription that was etched onto the card: "Dr. Gary Thompson, Registered Psychologist and Therapist." Was this a sign? Vicki had been pushing me to find someone to talk to for a long time, so maybe this was my chance to tell a professional how I was feeling about all the strange things I kept seeing.

• • •

Before going back to work the following week, I finally got up the courage to call Gary. The phone rang three times before going to voicemail. "Hello, you've reached Dr. Thompson. Please leave your name and number after the tone and I will get back to you as soon as possible." I debated hanging up, then took a deep breath and started, "Hi, Gary, um… I mean Dr. Thompson, it's Ellen Taylor. I hope you remember me, I'd like to schedule an appointment, so if you could please call me back, I'd appreciate it. Thank you." I left my home number and regretted not leaving my work number as well, just in case he called me when I was out. That day, after I came back from running a few errands, I was excited to see the little red light flashing on my answering machine. "Hi Ellen, it's Dr. Thompson… I mean Gary. Please give me a call anytime, even tonight if you'd like."

I changed into comfortable clothes and paced around the house, trying to convince myself that I was doing the right thing by calling him. Picking up the phone, my heartbeat sped up with each number key I touched. It rang twice, and just as I was about to hang up, he answered.

"Hello?" he said, his voice friendly and welcoming.

"Is this Dr. Thompson?" I said, my voice shaking.

"Yes, it is. Who's this?"

"Hi, it's Ellen Taylor returning your call. We met at your apartment a few weeks ago—" I paused, hoping he hadn't completely forgotten about me.

"Ellen, I've been worried about you. Are you okay?"

"I'm okay. Well, not really. Would it be possible to arrange a meeting?"

"Of course! Why don't you meet me at my place on Friday after work?" he suggested.

"Would seven o'clock be okay?" I replied, relieved that he didn't simply tell me to go away and hang up the phone.

"Works for me, see you then!"

I was anxious for the remainder of the week. As much as I looked forward to seeing him, I was worried that he might think I was completely insane. That night, as I slept soundly in bed, I woke up to the smell of cigarette smoke and, for the first time since my mother died, she appeared to me. She was sitting at the edge of my bed, looking healthy and smiling, holding her right arm out towards me. I tried to take her hand, but as soon as I reached for it, she disappeared.

• • •

The end of the week couldn't have come soon enough. I left work a bit earlier than usual, rushing home to shower, change my clothes, curl my hair, and put on some makeup, though I questioned why I did all of this—after all, this wasn't even a date, so what was I getting so worked up about?

When I got to Gary's place, I pressed the buzzer from the lobby. "Who is it?" he said on the other end of the speaker. "Hey, Gary, it's Ellen." The buzzer made a shrill nose that startled me and renewed my nerves.

"Hi, Ellen, you're trembling, is everything okay?" Gary asked when I reached his apartment.

"I'm okay, just a bit anxious I guess."

"No need to be nervous. Please come in, I'll make us some coffee."

"Actually, do you have anything stronger?"

"Glass of wine?"

"How about scotch?"

We sat in his living room, and all I could think about was the old woman I had encountered a few weeks ago, somehow I could still feel her presence.

"I'm glad you called me," he said, interrupting my thoughts as he handed me a full glass.

"Gary, I mean Dr. Thompson—"

"Please, call me Gary," he interrupted, clearly trying to make me feel more at ease.

"Gary, there is a lot going on in my life and I think I might need some help... if that's okay."

"Of course. I'll start by saying that whatever you tell me will stay between us. That's the same promise I give to all my clients."

We talked for just over two hours. I couldn't believe how easy it was to open up to him. He didn't judge me, I felt safe—and he never gave me those confused and judgmental looks like everyone else always did.

"I must say, you're an intriguing woman, Ellen."

"Do you think I'm crazy? Is there something wrong with me?"

"No, and no. But it's getting late, so we should continue this later. I think it's best if you come to my office next time. The setting is probably more appropriate." It sounded like he wanted to be my therapist and not my friend. Perhaps I scared him away with all of my stories, I thought, doubting myself again. "You can make an appointment with my assistant, the number is on my business card."

"Thank you, I'll do that," I responded, suddenly feeling uncomfortable. I left thinking that I might have made a huge mistake.

• • •

The next day, Vicki announced that she and Robert had set their wedding date for September seventeenth. "Sorry, Ellen, I know you were hoping we'd get married on your birthday, but we couldn't make it work. Hopefully you aren't too disappointed," Vicki said, looking hesitant to break this news to me. "No, of course not! I was joking, you know. I'm happy you guys finally set the date." I didn't have the heart to tell her that they chose the same date that Anna died. Vicki said she was going to arrange a blind date for me for the wedding, but I told her that I could never accept it, and then I mentioned Gary and said I was attracted to him. I wanted to see what she thought, but she seemed to doubt whether it would be possible to develop a relationship with him because he was my therapist. She did, however, seem to be very happy—and even relieved—that I finally consulted a professional.

• • •

After work that Thursday, I picked up my mail and noticed a white envelope with Paul's name written on the top left corner. My heart dropped. It had been months since I sent my letter, and I had given up hope that I would receive a response. My hands started shaking as I pulled the folded paper out of the envelope.

Dear Ellen,

I received your letter, and I was very happy when I did! I've been meaning to write you back for a while now, but things have been really busy and complicated lately. Everything seems to have settled down, and I'm in a much better place now.

I'll be in your area on business next month and would love to see you. If you're up for it, please give me a call.

Love, Paul.

P.S. I would've called you, but unfortunately I don't have your number.

I started crying, my tears spilling onto the letter like rain, making the ink run. I put the envelope on my living room table and decided to call him the next day.

When I got up the next morning, I went to look at the letter again, hardly believing that he had actually written me back, and as I picked it up, blood red drops trickled off the edge of it—it was almost like my tears had turned into blood. Was Anna trying to warn me about something? Still in my pyjamas, I went to Vicki's to show her tangible and undeniable evidence that I wasn't making these strange things up. She opened the door, half asleep, and hesitantly followed me to my apartment, still in her pyjamas, and then I showed her the letter.

"Could it be that you just had a paper cut on your finger that bled onto the letter when you put it back in the envelope?"

"There's nothing there, Vicki," I answered, holding out my hands, pointing to each one to make it obvious that there were no cuts anywhere. "I don't know how to explain this. I was planning on calling Paul today. I wonder if it's a bad sign."

"I don't think that's a good idea, Ellen," she said bluntly.

"Just be happy for me please. I need you to agree with me for once!" I snapped, growing impatient.

"Well… what can I say? Follow your heart, I guess."

"I need to see him one more time, Vicki. Even after all this time, I still need closure."

She nodded and gave me a hug before leaving, and then I took a deep breath and called Paul. When he picked up, he sounded surprised to hear my voice. We exchanged some pleasantries, and then arranged to meet when he would be in town. When we hung up, I pulled out a journal I had received as a birthday gift. I never knew what to write in it, but I figured this was as good a time as ever to start.

Dear Diary,

I'm feeling great today because I get to see my first love again! My best friend warned me that this might be a big mistake, but I need to know if there is any chance of Paul and I ever getting back together. I'm even ready to move to Vancouver with him if he asks. I can't stop thinking about him and I feel like there's no turning back now. I'm counting down the days until I get to see him again!

Everything will work out as it should
I cannot predict the future
I can only get ready for it
Will I be?

• • •

The following Friday, I got my hair done and bought a new outfit to wear for my date with Paul. I drove to the restaurant where we agreed to meet, arriving fifteen minutes early so I could calm my nerves and get comfortable. I waited in the parking lot, biting my nails in a hollow attempt to ease my anxiety. As I tilted my rear-view mirror to check my hair and makeup, I noticed the dream catcher ornament that I had hung off of it begin to swirl in circles, moving faster and faster. I grabbed it, but the minute I took my hands off it, it started spinning again. I tried to ignore it, unwilling to let anything cloud my mind before I met Paul. When I looked up, I saw him getting out of a cab. He looked exactly the same as he did when we met, but his hair was shorter now. His bright blue eyes still glistened in the sunlight and his strong features had become even more irresistible with age. I stepped out of my car as he walked towards me, unable to control my excited smile. "Hi, beautiful," he said, kissing me on the cheek. "It has been far too long." He took my hand, just like the old days, and we went inside.

The Venetian décor and paintings of the countryside on the walls displayed the tradition and charm of Italy. The hostess walked us to our table, and Paul pulled my chair back for me before he sat down. I think he could sense I was nervous because he ordered a bottle of wine right away and tried to break the ice with some small talk. After a few minutes, he told me that he had gone through a difficult separation with his ex, Judy, and that they shared a child together, named Johnathan. I almost fell off my chair, I definitely didn't expect that he'd have a son. I still imagined us as those young and naïve teenagers, sitting under our willow tree, hanging out at coffee shops, and riding our bikes everywhere because we didn't have a car. He fidgeted with his hands, I could tell he was struggling and felt uncomfortable, so I tried talking about something else, clumsily slipping into an even more awkward topic of conversation.

"Paul, what happened to us?" I asked. I didn't expect to ask this question so soon, but it came rushing out and I couldn't stop it.

Paul seemed surprised too, paused, then said, "Things changed, I guess. I mean, I loved you, I always will, but—"

"You broke my heart, Paul!" I interrupted. How could he be so casual about this? "You broke up with me without any explanation. You just left, and then I never saw you again. And then I had to find out that you were dating someone else? How could you do that to me?"

"I really am sorry for that, Ellen, there are no excuses for my actions. We—"

The waitress interrupted us, putting our desserts and coffees on the table, looking a bit alarmed at what she'd just walked into. When she left, we sat in silence for a few moments, each of us picking at the food on our plates.

"Ellen, there's something I need to tell you," he said, trying to alleviate the tension again.

"What is it, Paul?" I asked, sure that he was going to tell me he made a mistake and that he loved me and wanted us to get back together. But, as I looked at him, I could tell that this wasn't what he was going to say at all. "What's going on? You're scaring me."

"Well, there's no easy way to say this, so I guess I'll just cut right to the chase," he said, unable to look me in the eyes. "I'm gay, Ellen."

It felt like someone punched me in the stomach—this couldn't be happening. I hesitated, trying to figure out what the right way to respond to this was. "Since when? I mean, when did you know you were gay?"

"I know it's not what you wanted to hear—" he said, avoiding my question.

"Obviously not!" I interrupted, "I thought we were going to reconcile and maybe even start seeing each other again."

"I'm sorry, Ellen, but this is who I am, and I can't hide it anymore. When I told Judy... I mean... well, that was the reason for our separation."

"This is a joke, right? Please tell me it is!"

For days, I had been playing different versions of this night over and over in my head, but none of them went this way. Did he know this when we dated? Was our entire relationship a lie?

"It's not a joke, Ellen, I'm trying to be honest with you," he said, seeming to gain more confidence. "I didn't know for sure until years after I moved away, when I met a man and fell in love with him. I tried to resist it, believe me, but I am happy that I don't have to hide anymore."

I got up, unwilling to listen any longer. It wasn't that Paul was gay—I believed that people had the right to love whomever they chose—but it was the fact that he waited so long to tell me and made me question our entire relationship. I rushed through the doors of the restaurant, hearing Paul get up and run after me.

"I'm so sorry, Ellen," he said, holding my arm. He looked upset and defeated. "The last thing I ever wanted to do was hurt you. Please don't be mad... please just try to understand."

"I'm not mad, Paul. I just need some space. This is too much for me to handle right now," I answered, turning back as I raced to my car. I left him standing alone, looking vulnerable and heartbroken in the parking lot. I cried the whole way home—how could I have been so stupid? It felt like another door had just been slammed in my face. I cried myself to sleep, wondering if I'd ever catch a break and if I would ever be truly happy.

. . .

When I woke up the next morning, I felt like I had only slept for an hour. I grabbed the pillow to cover my eyes from the sun as its bright rays cascaded through the blinds. All I wanted was to block out the world for a little while longer. I started thinking about everything that Paul told me the night before, when I felt something tickling my arm. At first, I thought it could be a bug, but when I looked closer, I saw a strand of Anna's golden hair resting on my forearm. "Thanks Anna!" I said, convinced that she left it there to let me know she was with me. I picked it up and placed it in the box where I stored the other locks I had found, and then I went to the bathroom to look at myself in the mirror. I was barely recognizable—my eyelids were swollen like balloons and my face was covered in red dots that I usually got when I was stressed. I looked just as bad as I felt.

No matter what I did, I couldn't stop thinking about Paul. I tried to remember the times we were together to see if I might have overlooked the clear signals that would have revealed his secret. Sure, he was delicate, sensitive, and kind, but that's what I loved about him. I called Vicki for support, but she didn't answer, so I decided to go for a walk to clear my head. After I changed my clothes and put on my running shoes, I opened my front door, and found Vicki coming up the stairs. I immediately threw myself into her arms and started crying.

"What's wrong? Is it Paul?" she asked, looking deeply concerned. I invited her in and poured us two cups of coffee. We sat at the table in silence for a moment, then I went through every heartbreaking detail of the previous night. I always wondered why Derek—the guy Vicki and I met at the bar on my twenty-second birthday— was so insistent that I call Paul, he probably knew about this!

"Jesus! I can't believe this!" she screamed. "See?! I told you not to call him! This is crazy!" I could tell she enjoyed the gossip and couldn't really comprehend the degree to which this hurt me, but I needed the company.

• • •

Later that night, I wrote Paul a letter so that I could finally say everything I didn't have the chance to the night before.

Dear Paul,

I am sorry for how I reacted and for the way I left you at the restaurant. You didn't deserve that, but you caught me off-guard and I didn't know what to say. I guess I just needed some time to deal with my emotions privately.

Thank you for opening up to me, I know that must have been really hard for you. I want you to be happy and, no matter what, nothing will ever erase the memories I have of you and of us.

I wish you happiness in your life. Next time you're in town, please call me. I'd really like us to be friends.

Love,
Ellen

CHAPTER FIFTEEN

MOVING ON

I tied a dream catcher above my bed, hoping that it would trap my bad dreams and protect me during the night. My efforts were in vain, however, because that same night I was woken up by scratching noises coming from the corner of my room. When I looked over, I saw the dark figure hovering near my dresser, slowly moving closer towards me. I sat upright, screaming at the top of my lungs, and, to my surprise, it disappeared. It didn't matter that I had burned sage and opened all my windows, that evil thing kept stalking me. I felt lost and confused and was in constant sorrow. Everything in my life seemed so strange and inexplicable, and I longed to be normal and find my way out of this crazy maze.

I remembered the time my mother said that playing outside would take my mind off things. Maybe she was right, perhaps I needed to change up my routine. I thought about Harry's invitation and planned on going to the North Pub that weekend. When I got there, I sat alone at a small table in the corner, hoping he wouldn't see me as he serenaded the audience. Listening to him sing and play his guitar transported me back to our time in Mexico, where everything was so carefree and tranquil. Halfway through his set, he glanced over at me and smiled before calling me onstage for the big finale. "Ladies and gentlemen, I'd like to introduce a friend of mine, Ellen Taylor! She's a talented singer and guitarist," he told the audience, making it impossible for me to decline his request. The audience started clapping and I felt my face turn bright red as I timidly stood up and made my way to the stage. Harry handed me an acoustic guitar, and I plucked up the courage and started playing with him. We did a few songs and it felt like we had been doing this together all our lives.

After we finished, we got a drink and then, at the end of the evening, he walked me to my car and put his arms around me, whispering, "We should do this again, Ellen. I think we're a great match." Then he leaned closer and tried to kiss me, but I pushed him away. "You're a nice guy, Harry, and I like you a lot, but just as a friend. My life is a bit complicated, and to be honest, my heart belongs to someone else right now."

He blushed. "I'm sorry Ellen, I feel like a fool," he said quickly, fixing his eyes on the ground. "I don't know what came over me. You're just so beautiful, smart, and talented, so I'd be lying if I said I wasn't attracted to you... but I shouldn't have crossed the line. I'm sorry, can you forgive me?"

"No worries, Harry. It's okay!" I answered, smiling back. He had always been so nice to me, and I knew his intentions were innocent.

He asked if I wanted to come back onstage with him next weekend, but I declined, saying that I found it way too stressful, then we hugged and went our separate ways. I wondered if part of the reason I didn't want to get close to Harry was because he reminded me so much of Paul, or maybe it was because I couldn't get Gary out of my head. Either way, I wasn't in the proper head-space to deal with another man in my life.

• • •

When I got home and opened my apartment door, the pungent smell of roses mixed with perfume and cigarettes pervaded the room. I entered slowly and heard the television, which I was certain I had turned off before leaving. I put my purse down and walked to the living room, filled with trepidation, wondering what was waiting for me this time. When I turned the corner, I saw five figures sitting on my couch, all of them dressed in white, with pale skin and blood-red coloured lips. My heart began racing, not because I was terrified—they didn't look threatening to me—but more from excitement and adrenaline. When I calmed down and focused my eyes, I saw Anna, her mother, my mother, and the old lady from Gary's apartment, but I didn't recognize the fifth figure. She was small and sad looking, but I was almost certain that she was the same woman who frequently appeared with Anna after she died.

I stood in front of them, waiting for something to happen, but they stayed silent, keeping their eyes fixated on me. "Well, are you going to say something? Why are all of you here?" I demanded impatiently. I heard a few mumbles that sounded like, "Be careful," but they wouldn't say anything else. "Will you please tell me what I need to be careful of?" I insisted, hoping that this time I'd finally get an answer. I took my eyes off them for a split second, and when I looked back again, they had disappeared. I turned to go back to the kitchen, when I noticed that some of the things on my side table had been moved. I walked over to it—the plant, candles, and picture frames were all arranged in a perfectly straight line, and sitting on the end was the gold necklace that Jack had given me for my birthday. I vividly remembered throwing it out, as clearly as if it had happened yesterday. Jack was still in prison, there's no way he could have put it there. Maybe my mind was playing tricks on me, there had to be a reasonable explanation for all of this. I moved to my room, exhausted and confused, and turned on all the lights before going to sleep, hoping this would protect me from all these visitors of the night.

• • •

That Sunday, I went to the store to buy some milk—any excuse to drive by Gary's place. I stopped on the side of the road, trying to convince myself that I should visit him. It would be breaking the rules, I knew that, but my desire to see him was stronger than following any rules. I needed his help—or maybe more like his empathy. I took the brush out of my purse to comb my hair, then put on some lipstick and tucked in my shirt to make myself look presentable. I got out of my car, and eagerly approached his building, before buzzing his apartment from the lobby. I felt like I waited an eternity, my heart racing, so I hit the buzzer again. Just as I was about to leave, I heard his voice over the intercom. "Hello? Who is it?" My voice clung in my throat. "It's Ellen, I know I shouldn't be here but—" the intercom cut off, and then the door clicked open. In the elevator, I pressed the number seven, and was overcome by a string of flashbacks, which heightened my anxiety.

When Gary opened the door, he leaned on the frame, grinning at me, his unshaven face making him look even more handsome. "What's up, Ellen?" he asked casually.

I blushed at the way he looked at me. "I… uh… I was hoping we could talk," I stuttered.

"I'm happy to see you, Ellen, but as your therapist this could get me in trouble."

"What if I told you that you are no longer my therapist?"

"What do you mean?"

"Exactly what I said. You're no longer my therapist!"

"Okay… would you like me to refer you to someone else?" he frowned, failing to understand what I was implying.

"Maybe, but right now I just need a friend."

"In that case, I accept," he said, inviting me in.

We walked down the long hallway and sat on the couch next to each other, the surroundings were all too familiar to me. Before he could utter another word, I broke down and told him what happened with Paul. I could tell he felt badly for me, and his presence was so comforting.

"I can understand how this must have come as a shock to you, Ellen. How are you dealing with it?" he asked in a tone that seemed detached and diagnostic.

"Please stop talking to me like you're my therapist, just tell it like it is!"

He rolled up his sleeves and ran his hand through his hair, "Okay then. This sucks. It really does!" We both burst out laughing.

He got up to make coffee and, when he returned, he sat closer to me than he did before, placing his arm around my shoulders. I turned my head to look at him, and our eyes locked before I leaned over and kissed him on the cheek. He looked like he was caught off-guard, and pulled back. "Oh gosh, I'm so sorry, Gary, I shouldn't have—" He put his index over my lips to shush me, and then he pulled me towards him and kissed me passionately.

The next thing I knew, we were on his bed and he was unbuttoning my shirt, his eyes moving with purpose and intention. I felt like my heart was about to explode when he removed my pants, before he took his clothes off. "You are so beautiful, Ellen," he said, kissing me sensually up and down my neck. I wanted him more than I ever wanted anyone before. We made love, and I wished that it would never end.

"You're trembling, Ellen, are you okay?" he asked after. I was self-conscious, I'm sure he could sense it. He pulled me in even closer and held me tight.

"Was this okay?" he said, hopeful.

"Okay? Are you kidding me? It was amazing!" I answered, throwing my hands up in the air.

"So, what do we do now?" he asked.

"Well… before we do anything, I need to use the bathroom," I giggled.

"Down the hallway, first door on your left, but of course, you know that already."

I took my shirt off the floor and headed for the bathroom. As I walked down the hallway, I jumped when I saw the old lady standing by the door, glaring at me. I screamed and Gary came running.

"Ellen, what's wrong?"

"You said you didn't know the old lady! What is she doing here, Gary?"

"What are you talking about? There's no one there!"

"She's standing right there!" I yelled, pointing at her.

"Ellen, trust me, there's no one here but us."

I started feeling faint and dizzy, losing my balance and toppling against the wall. Gary looked deeply concerned, and poured me a glass of water before sitting me down on the couch.

"I'm sorry. You must think I'm losing my mind," I said, regaining my composure.

"No, I don't. You're going through a lot right now, Ellen. This type of reaction is completely understandable. The old lady you saw… are you sure she's the same person you drove here a few weeks ago?"

"Yes, I'm positive," I said, sobbing.

"Okay, sweetie, but maybe she's just a figment of your imagination… a manifestation of your anxiety and past trauma."

"Of course you would say that! I don't expect you to believe me, no one does!" I cried. Gary put his arms around me and held me until I calmed down. There was something so comforting about his embrace, and I knew that no matter what, I didn't ever want to let him go.

• • •

Over the next few weeks, Gary and I started seeing each other more and more. He was there for me when I needed him most, to console me when I felt lost, to protect me when I was afraid. We often spent the night together, and he frequently woke me from my nightmares. When he heard me talking to Anna, he never judged me or questioned what was happening. He even witnessed one of my out-of-body experiences. I had warned him that these happened sometimes, and told him never to wake me up because I might not be able to re-enter my body—I read that some people never wake up after something like that and that they remained in a coma for the rest of their lives. I don't know how he put up with all my baggage. If the roles were reversed, I doubt I could do the same. As time went on, I truly started to believe that he was sent to me from heaven.

• • •

For my twenty-sixth birthday, Gary took me for a romantic weekend to New York, and we stayed at a beautiful hotel in Manhattan. On our first night there, we went to see a show on Broadway and had dinner at a five-star restaurant. I felt so lucky and spoiled. The next day, we took a walk in Central Park, I was awestruck by its beauty and history—I could feel the ghosts around me, whispering their stories and making their presence known. "Let's have a seat and admire the beautiful view," Gary said, leading me over to a park bench. He put his arm around me and said, "I know it's only been a few months, but it feels like we've been together forever. I love you so much, Ellen." It was like something out of a movie. I grinned at him, wanting to pinch myself to make sure this was real. "What do you say we move in together?" he continued, taking me by surprise. I wasn't expecting it to happen so soon, but we practically lived together already.

"I would love that!" I said, kissing him on the cheek.

"Maybe it would make more sense to buy a house. Renting seems like such a big waste of money."

"Well that's definitely something we can discuss… if we can afford it," I answered, trying to conceal my reservations. I wasn't afraid of commitment, but money had always been a concern for me, and I didn't have enough to contribute for a down payment. He told me not to worry, that his money was our money and we'd find a way to make it work.

On our way home from the airport, we picked up a couple of real estate brochures and read through every page during dinner with excitement. We found a ranch-style home we both liked, and Gary called the real estate agent to book an appointment to see it that week. My heart was full, I never felt happier. On Tuesday after work, we met the realtor at the house—coincidently, the house number was seventy-seven. I loved the area, it was close to my father's house and in a quiet rural area. I fell in love with the wrap around porch and, though it wasn't very big, it seemed spacious and airy and more than enough room for us—and even a child someday. The master bedroom featured a large bay window that showcased the tall pine trees and beautiful garden in the backyard.

"This is the one, I can feel it! Let's buy it!" I proclaimed, jumping up and down.

"If you like it, then let's do it!"

I leapt into his arms and wrapped my legs around his waist. "I love you!" I shouted as I kissed his face.

We made an official offer on the house that evening, and the realtor said we would have to wait a couple of days before we heard back because the owners were out of town.

. . .

Later, when we got back to my place, we knocked on Vicki and Robert's door to share our news. Robert opened the door, his eyes all puffy and red.

"Are you okay, Robert?" I asked.

"I tried to call you. Vicki was rushed to the hospital this evening."

"What? What happened? Is she okay?"

"She had excruciating pain in her abdomen… they found a large cyst and had to operate on her right away, and when they opened her up—" he paused, crying so hard he couldn't speak.

"What is it, Robert, you're scaring me," I demanded, hyperventilating.

"They had to remove her uterus," he answered, his voice trembling.

"Oh, Robert, I am so sorry!" I said, giving him a hug. "How is she doing?" I asked.

"She's okay, but of course she's inconsolable. She wanted children so badly, but—"

"Can we go see her?" I interrupted, not wanting to be apart from her for a moment longer.

Robert told us that he was sent home because visiting hours were over for the night. I barely slept at all, wishing that I could be there for my friend. I couldn't imagine how she must be feeling.

. . .

The next morning, I rushed to the hospital, and my heart broke when I saw her lying on her hospital bed, frail and as white as a ghost. I pulled a chair next to her bed, and took her hand.

"How are you doing, best friend? I'm so sorry this happened."

"I will never be able to have children, Ellen," she said, tearing up. Her tone expressed her heartbreak, and I could tell that everything that happened still hadn't fully registered in her mind.

"I know, I'm so sorry, Vicki, but this doesn't mean you can never be a mother. You can still adopt, right?"

As soon as I said this, I immediately regretted it—it was too soon to bring this up. She gave me a stern look and started wailing. I knew it wasn't the right time to tell her my news, so I stayed quiet and sat with her for a few more hours. She told me that she and Robert still planned on getting married to add some joy to this devastating turn of events, but that they'd postpone their honeymoon to the Poconos until February.

• • •

Vicki came back from the hospital the following Thursday, two days before her wedding. Luckily, she was able to stand up for her vows, but she stayed seated for the rest of the ceremony. During the reception, we told them about our house—our offer had been accepted and we planned to move in November—and they were excited for us.

"Maybe we'll get a house in the same neighbourhood as you guys. Right, Robert?" said Vicki, excitedly.

"Anything you want, my love," Robert replied as he kissed her.

Vicki looked at me and said, "How lucky are we to have found such handsome and amazing men?" She could not be more right about that, I thought.

After we left the reception, Gary and I visited the cemetery, and I placed a pink rose on Anna's grave. I found myself missing her more than ever, wishing that I could tell her everything that was going on in my life. I told Gary all about Anna—what she looked like, the fond memories I had of her, and how she tragically died so long ago—and felt all the more connected to him for sharing this important part of my past.

• • •

When we got back to my place later that night, we went straight to bed, and as soon as I fell asleep, I had a vivid dream about the house with the seven doors again. "Please open that door, there must be a way, there has to be!" I screamed, when I reached the end. I felt a jolt and woke up to Gary gently shaking my arm and rubbing my back.

"Are you okay, sweetie?" he asked, looking concerned. He got up to get me a glass of water and we sat in bed for a while, and he asked me to describe the little boy I saw.

"He's seven years old, with dark hair and big brown eyes, and about four feet tall. He always wears a white shirt with black pants."

"And what about you?" he asked, as if knowing the details would help him interpret my dream.

"Well, I can tell that I'm also around the same age, and we're about the same height. When I look down, I'm always wearing a yellow dress, the one I had on the day Anna died, and there are drops of blood all over it."

He looked puzzled, unsure of what to say, but I was grateful that, no matter how crazy my stories seemed, he was always there to take care of me and talk me through it.

CHAPTER SIXTEEN

A NEW MYSTERY

We moved into our new house on a crisp and breezy November afternoon. The trees were skirted with gold and rust coloured leaves that swirled in the wind like small tornados. Gary rented a moving van, and then he and Robert drove to his place to pick up his things. I stayed at my apartment with Vicki, who helped me pack the last-minute odds and ends, as we shared memories of the good times we'd had there together. Vicki was the one constant person in my life, she was always there for me through thick and thin, and I was so grateful to have her as my best friend. As we finished packing up the last box, she told me that she and Robert bought a house within fifteen-minutes walking distance from my new home, though she said they wouldn't move in until March. I jumped up and down in excitement—and I was relieved that we'd remain close even after I moved in with Gary.

Once we cleaned up, I looked out the window and saw the moving van pull into the parking lot. "They're here!" I shouted, taking a deep breath before embarking on my new adventure. Gary walked in with Robert and two of his friends, and less than an hour later the place was empty and we were ready to go. Before we left, I took one last look around to make sure I hadn't left anything behind. When I got to my bedroom and opened the closet door, I was hit by a breeze that was so cold that I could see my breath. I scanned the closet, shivering, and saw my Ouija board tucked away in the far-left corner of the upper shelf, so I picked it up and hid it under my jacket to make sure no one would notice it. When I got back outside, Vicki asked what I was hiding inside my jacket. "Oh… it's just a picture frame I found in my closet," I lied. "I'll just bring it with me separately." I rushed over to the car and quickly threw the Ouija board in the trunk, praying that Vicki wouldn't catch me.

At the new house, Gary and Robert unloaded the van while Vicki and I unpacked a few of the boxes inside. After a long day, we ordered pizza and enjoyed a well-deserved break. Later, when everyone left, I looked at Gary and said, "How is it possible that I still find you so irresistible even with your messy hair, scruffy beard, and dirty clothes?" He let out a deep laugh from his belly. "Ah!" he said as he pulled me closer. "That must be what unconditional love is all about!"

After we settled in, we showered and put on our pajamas. "We did it!" I exclaimed, falling onto the couch, exhausted. "We sure did, and I've never been happier," Gary said, as he walked to the entrance closet and pulled out a bouquet of flowers to surprise me. I almost felt guilty that I hadn't bought anything for him to celebrate our new home. "To new beginnings, my love," he said, handing me the flowers and giving me a hug.

We decided to snuggle on the couch and watch television for the rest of the evening. An hour later, Gary stood up unexpectedly and took my hands and pulled me towards him. "Gary, what's going on?" I asked, confused. Then, he lowered himself onto one knee, my heart pounding as I anticipated his next move, and pulled out a small blue velvet box from his pocket.

"Ellen, my sweet Ellen, will you be mine forever?"

"Oh my God! Are you serious?"

He laughed nervously and said, "Of course I'm serious! Is that a yes?"

"I can't imagine growing old with anyone else but you, baby. Yes, yes. I love you!"

"I think we should plan our wedding for September," Gary said, as he took my hand and put the ring on my finger, its seven diamonds sparkling in the light. "We both love the fall and it would be so special to get married on your twenty-seventh birthday."

I leapt off the couch excitedly and called Vicki to share my news and ask her to be my maid of honour. "Are you kidding me? I wouldn't have it any other way!" she said, before she started talking about what we would do for my bachelorette party. That night before going to sleep, I wrote four words in my diary:

I am getting married!

• • •

A week later, I woke up feeling well-rested and refreshed as I looked out my bedroom window and saw the trees covered in a thick, white blanket—a bit early, I thought. I always loved the first snowfall, and even more so that year because it would be our first Christmas in our new home. Vicki came over for lunch, marvelling at my new aqua-blue wing chairs in the living room. "I love the ocean blues and cream décor in this room, Ellen. It gives me some good ideas for my new house," she said. I could sense that she wasn't herself and noticed her eyes filling up with tears.

"Is everything okay?" I asked, not wanting to press her too hard.

She was silent. "The truth is that the adoption process is killing me," she finally said, looking guilty. "I'm starting to question whether we should even go through with it."

"I understand. I can't imagine how hard it must be, but I don't think you should give up. You're going to be such an amazing mother, Vicki!"

"I hope so."

"What do you mean?"

"Well, I'm sure I'll be a better parent than my adoptive father was."

"What? What do you mean?" I asked again, confused.

"I'm adopted, Ellen… but you already knew that, right?"

"How could I have known that? You've never mentioned anything about this to me before," I said, grinning slightly, thinking that she might be joking.

"Haven't you ever wondered why I don't look anything like my parents?"

"I mean… I guess. But I didn't want to assume anything."

"Well now you know!"

"What did you mean by your comment about your father?"

"He wasn't a nice man, Ellen. He was abusive to me and my mother for years."

"I'm so sorry, Vicki. I knew something wasn't right when I saw him running after your mother with a knife when we were young… and when I saw those bruises all over your body, but I didn't know how bad it really was. Why didn't you ever talk to me about this back then?"

"I couldn't, he made me promise never to tell anyone. He threatened my mother and me. That was such a hard time, I'm so happy that my mother was so good to me."

"Oh God, I should have picked up on that. I'm so sorry, Vicki," I said, tears starting to well up in my eyes.

"Remember that one time when you came to my house and my father said I was sleeping? The truth is that he hit me with his belt buckle so hard that I had marks on my body for weeks," she confessed, sobbing as she relived these painful memories.

"That's awful! Your father is a monster!"

"I don't refer to him as my father anymore. He's just someone who agreed to adopt me because my mother really wanted a child."

This revelation broke my heart. I felt so helpless and didn't know what to say, so I tried to change the conversation to a happier topic.

"Shall we go Christmas shopping next Saturday?"

Vicki ignored my proposal. "Ellen, I have a question, and please be honest."

"I'm always honest, Vicki, what is it?"

"Did you get rid of the Ouija board?" she asked, giving me her signature stern look.

"Not yet, but I will," I answered, remembering that I had left it in my car.

"Ellen, you need to get rid of it now. I don't want you to invite evil into your new home. Please listen to me this time!" she pled.

"Don't worry about it, it'll be fine," I replied in a tone that made her request seem trivial.

As soon as she drove off, I rushed to my car to get the Ouija board out of the trunk. Dusk had swept in and covered the sky with thick clouds that extinguished the light. I struggled with my car keys, and when I finally unlocked the trunk, I reached in for the board and felt something grab a hold of my arm, trying to pull me in. I pulled my arm back, and ran a few feet away from the car. I slowly walked back towards it, telling myself that this was all in my imagination, and then I saw that the board had been taken out of its box. It was lying open on the trunk floor, the pointer moving back and forth between the letters Z and O. As I stared at it in disbelief, I felt a finger trace its way up my hand and along my forearm. I leapt back, falling to the ground, and when I got up, I slammed the trunk closed before running into the house.

When I got back inside, I curled up on the couch, covered myself in a blanket, and waited for Gary to come home. When he finally pulled up into the driveway, I rushed to the front and threw myself into his arms as soon as he came through the door.

"What's wrong, sweetie?" he asked, looking alarmed.

"Nothing, I just missed you, that's all," I lied, crying uncontrollably.

"That much, eh? Don't cry, I'm here now!"

When we went to bed that night, he noticed two bruises the size of quarters on my right arm, just above my elbow.

"What's this? What happened to you?"

"Oh, that... it's probably from me moving those chairs around earlier today."

"That's odd," he said, frowning.

"Not really. I bruise easily. Don't worry about it," I lied again.

I'm not sure he believed me, but he didn't persist.

• • •

My family came over for Christmas dinner—Gary's parents lived in Michigan, so we hardly ever saw them. My father arrived, still looking like a classic sixties business man, though he used to have a full head of black hair and now he was bald on top and grey on his temples. His eyes were his strongest feature, and everyone always commented on them. They were big and round, and the colour of light green grape raisins. He looked at people straight in their eyes, it was almost like he could see right through them. He came with a woman clinging to his arm, introducing her as Rita, his neighbour, who was also a widow. "Nice to meet you Rita," I said, as I gave her a welcoming hug. She seemed nice, soft spoken with a friendly smile, and modestly dressed. He seemed happy, more so than I had seen since my mother passed away. Dinner turned out to be a full-on feast, and everyone enjoyed the food, which made me proud given that it was my first time cooking such a large meal.

. . .

The next day, Vicki and Robert invited us over for dinner at their place. We decided to take my car and, when Gary walked around the back to put the gifts in the trunk, I panicked and shouted, "No! Wait!" trying to hide the Ouija board that was locked inside. I sprinted over to help defend him against whatever evil waited there, but when I got closer, I discovered that the board was gone.

"Uh... is everything okay, Ellen?" Gary asked, giving me a strange and almost comical look. "You're acting kind of weird."

"Oh, it's nothing. I just thought I forgot something in the trunk," I answered, concealing how afraid I really was.

When we arrived, Vicki immediately sensed that something was wrong, but she didn't ask what was going on in front of Gary and Robert. We ate dinner, had good conversation and a few laughs and then, when we were done, Vicki suggested that she and I go for a walk.

"Ellen, what's going on with you? I know there's something you're not telling me," she insisted, as soon as we started walking down the street.

"I'm scared Vicki. It's... well it's the Ouija board," I confessed. I told her that something tried to pull me into the trunk, and that the board had disappeared when I looked before we left the house that day. I wasn't sure if she would believe me, but I had to say something about it, I just couldn't keep it to myself anymore.

"Seriously, Ellen? Are you ever going to listen to me? That thing is evil and it's got to go!" she screeched.

"Okay, but I don't know where it is. It was in my car, but it's not there anymore!"

"Well it didn't just grow legs and walk away! Did Gary take it?"

"No, I'm pretty sure he didn't."

"Okay, this is insane," she said, growing increasingly frustrated. "Maybe you brought it inside and now you don't remember."

"No, I didn't, Vicki. But I promise, I will get rid of it as soon as I find it."

Where the hell could it be?

. . .

When I left for work the next morning, I had the urge to check the trunk again, but I held back—a new lawyer was joining the firm that day, and I didn't want to be late or distracted for my first meeting with him. When I got to the office, I noticed his name plate, reading "Anthony Edmonds," already fixed to the office door across from my desk. I couldn't help myself, I counted the number of letters in his first and last name—seven in each! I started working and it felt like someone was watching me. "Hello, Miss Taylor," said a raspy and deep voice. I looked up and saw a tall man with dark hair, chocolate brown eyes, and an expensive blue designer suit.

"You must be Mr. Edmonds," I said as I stood up to shake his hand.

"Please call me Anthony," he said rubbing his fingers through his full head of hair.

"Okay, but only if you call me Ellen," I smiled.

We seemed to hit it off right away and, after chatting for a while, I felt like I knew him, but I didn't know from where.

"Have we met before?" I asked finally, unable to take the mystery any longer.

"No, I don't think so," he answered with wondering eyes.

He told me that he wasn't from the area and that he had just moved in for the job, but something about him still seemed very familiar. In the afternoon, I went to his office and asked if he wanted a coffee, telling him that I was going to go get one for myself at the coffee shop on the main floor. "Actually, if you don't mind, I'll go with you," he answered, grabbing his suit jacket and swinging it over his shoulder. This was the perfect opportunity to get to know him better.

We sat at a small table in the corner of the coffee shop and, a few minutes into our conversation, I discovered that we were the same age. I tried to find out more about him and his family, but he wouldn't reveal much, other than that he had an older sister, whom he rarely ever saw because she lived in Chicago. "Hey, you'd make a good detective," he said, laughing at my endless string of questions. "I'm sorry, Anthony, I didn't mean to pry. I'm just trying to figure out where we might have met before," I answered, my face turning red. "Well, anything is possible, but I don't think we have, Ellen," he said, before changing the subject—but in my mind I was unwilling to let this go.

CHAPTER SEVENTEEN
PATCH

Spring was in the air—a season of new beginnings, when the earth comes alive again. The flower beds in my backyard seemed to bloom overnight, proud to showcase their bright colours and sweet fragrances. I sat on our patio at a bistro table that we placed under a picturesque cherry blossom tree, taking in the sun and warm breeze. Gary had gone out to help a friend build a deck, so I stayed outside drinking sweet lemonade all afternoon, with the butterfly on my shoulder keeping me company. I started to doze off and was startled when it fluttered away and landed on my nose, looking me straight in the eye, before disappearing from my line of sight. "Anna, if you can hear me, please help me figure out what happened to the Ouija board," I said out loud, but received no response. I suddenly felt nauseous and sprinted to the bathroom— maybe I got too much sun, I thought.

• • •

Gary came home later that afternoon and joined me on the patio, holding two bottles of beer in his hands. My stomach was still a little bit off, so I told him that I'd rather have water, and then he grilled a couple of burgers on the barbecue. We ate outside and discussed our wedding, agreeing to keep it small and intimate. I suggested that we have the ceremony in the small church where I grew up because it meant a lot to me and I knew that it would have made my mother happy. Everything seemed to be going exceptionally well, yet I couldn't help but wonder if it was all too good to be true.

We went for a walk after dinner and stopped at Vicki and Robert's house for tea. They were all settled into their new place, and Vicki gave us an update on their adoption, saying that the agency told them that they could become parents sooner if they considered international adoption. "Every child deserves a family, no matter which part of the world they come from," I said, as Vicki nodded in agreement. As the night wore on, I started feeling so tired that I could barely keep my eyes open. "Time to go, sweetie?" Gary said with a wink, noticing that I was falling asleep in my chair.

When we got home, I went directly to bed and slept through the night. Early the next morning, I opened my eyes, feeling like I was spinning at a thousand miles an hour. I ran to the bathroom, and when Gary heard me throwing up, he tapped cautiously on the bathroom door.

"Ellen, are you okay?" he asked, opening the door and poking his head inside.

"I don't know what's wrong with me," I groaned, keeled over on the floor.

"You're as white as a ghost, you don't look well at all, sweetie," he said, crouching down beside me and placing his hand on my forehead. "Doesn't feel like you have a fever though."

"My stomach has been off since yesterday. I think I just need more sleep," I answered, slowly picking myself up off the floor. I hobbled back to bed and Gary brought me a glass of water, before closing the door quietly behind him.

"How are you feeling?" he asked, checking on me an hour later.

"Better, but now I'm hungry!" I answered, stretching out my arms across the bed.

"That's my girl! I made soup and ham sandwiches, if you're up for it."

I followed him to the kitchen, still in my pyjamas, and ate every morsel of food he placed in front of me. We spent the rest of the day cozied up on the couch, watching old black and white movies. Even though I started to feel better, I went to bed early, falling asleep as soon as my head hit the pillow. I dreamt about the hallway with the seven doors, and the little boy looking at me with eyes as sharp as laser beams, and although I could see his lips moving, I couldn't hear anything he said. A dark, sinister feeling came over me, as I plummeted out of my dreamscape, and I sat straight up in bed, "Someone died in there!" I yelled, covered in sweat.

"Ellen, what's going on?" Gary asked, rushing into the bedroom. "You scared the crap out of me!"

"I'm okay, I had that dream again, about the house and that long hallway—"

"I'm sorry. I'm here, sweetie. Everything is okay, try to go back to sleep," he said, rubbing my shoulders to calm me down.

• • •

The next morning, I woke up early and, as soon as my feet hit the floor, I was overcome by nausea and ran to the bathroom. "Ellen, I think it's time for you to see a doctor, maybe you have a stomach bug or something," Gary said, coming in and sitting down on the floor beside me. I took a cold shower to try to get rid of my dizziness, then got dressed and went to the kitchen. The last thing I felt like doing was going to work, but I had no choice—Anthony scheduled a meeting for that morning and I couldn't miss it.

I drove to the office, keeping the windows down, hoping the breeze would keep me from feeling motion sickness, and when I got there a few minutes early, Anthony was busily working at his desk. We went for coffee before the meeting, and, as we talked, I still couldn't shake the feeling that I had met him before.

We went back to the office and, as I sat in the meeting room listening to Anthony's presentation, I began to feel sick to my stomach, so I excused myself and went to the bathroom and stayed there for the rest of the meeting. Later, Anthony called me into his office and asked if I was okay. I told him it was just indigestion, but these symptoms were starting to scare me, and I couldn't figure out what was wrong. Before I left work, I called the doctor's office and made an appointment for the following day.

. . .

When I finally pulled into the driveway a few hours later, Gary was outside waiting for me.

"Hurry, I have a surprise for you, sweetie," he said excitedly.

"You do? But it's not my birthday!"

"Ah! A man doesn't need an excuse to surprise his lady, does he?"

"What is it? I can't wait!"

"Close your eyes."

He put his hand over my eyes and led me inside the house.

"Okay, you can open them now," he said when we got there.

"Oh my God! A cat, you got us a cat! Thank you, thank you, thank you, baby!" I cried, looking down at a small, black cat with a white spot of fur on his back.

I jumped up and down with joy, I had wanted a cat ever since I was a child, but my parents never let me get one.

"I got him from the animal shelter. I passed by on my way home from work and, when I saw him, I just couldn't resist getting him for you."

"He's perfect, I love him! Let's call him Patch. That white fur on his back is so cute," I grinned, happy to welcome a new member into our family.

Even though it was a beautiful evening, we ate dinner inside because we didn't want to leave Patch alone. I picked at my food, having no appetite for anything, and Gary asked if I had called the doctor. I told him that I booked an appointment for the next day, and he made me promise to call him right after to give him an update.

As we sat, discussing how our days went, Patch took off to explore the house, inspecting every room and hidden corner he could find. After we finished cleaning up, I followed him around and chuckled at the little squeaks he made each time he discovered something new, like he was trying to tell me something. I leaned over to pick him up and take him back to the living room, and he began hissing at me, before running down the hall. I thought that perhaps something scared him, or maybe he didn't like being picked up, though he didn't seem to mind when Gary did.

That night, Patch slept in our bed, and at three in the morning, I woke up feeling like I was being watched. When I opened my eyes, the cat was standing beside my right shoulder, staring at me intensely, and suddenly I felt my chest tightening and struggled to breathe. I sat upright, gasping for air, thinking that I might be having an anxiety attack. The commotion woke Gary up, and he tried to calm me down. "I know it's silly, sweetie, but I'd feel better if the cat didn't sleep in our bedroom," Gary said. "Maybe you have some allergies we didn't know about, and that's why you can't breathe." He swiftly scooped up the cat and put him outside, shutting the door behind him.

• • •

When I opened the door in the morning, I expected Patch to come running in, but to my surprise, he was nowhere to be found. I put my robe on and went looking for him around the house, but I couldn't find him anywhere.

"Did you let the cat out of the house?" I asked, running back into the bedroom and shaking Gary awake.

"No, of course not. Why?" he asked, rubbing his eyes.

"I looked everywhere, and I can't find him."

"That's strange, I'm sure he's just hiding. I'll go look for him."

He checked every corner of the house, and found Patch hidden under the couch in the living room.

"But I just looked there, I swear!" I exclaimed when he came back into the room, carrying the cat in his right hand.

"Cats move around, sweetie, they're pretty clever that way," he answered, confused about why I was so alarmed.

"I don't think he likes me."

"Don't be silly, he's just doing what cats do."

I showered and drove to my doctor's appointment, and when I got there, I fidgeted in the waiting room for half an hour, anticipating my turn. I jumped out of my chair when I heard my name being called by a nurse, dressed in a pink uniform. "Ms. Taylor, the doctor will see you now," she announced in a happy, high-pitched voice. She handed me a medical gown and asked me to sit on the exam table, where I waited for another ten minutes. As I looked around the room at all the medical equipment, I felt anxious and scared, until Dr. Grace finally walked in the room.

"Hello, Ellen, what brings you here today?" she asked in a friendly tone.

"It's probably nothing, but I keep throwing up, and I have no energy," I answered.

She ran through her list of questions, and then told me to lie down on the table, as she palpated my stomach and asked if it hurt anywhere she was pressing. "I'd like to run some more tests and take some blood, just to make sure that everything is okay," she said, as she put on a pair of medical rubber gloves. When she was done, she instructed me to get dressed and meet her in her office.

"Alright, I think I know what's going on here, Ellen," she said calmly when I entered and took a seat, holding my breath. "Congratulations! You're pregnant! You're about four weeks along!"

I stared at her in shock for a few moments, unsure of how I should react. This was the last thing I expected to hear—it wasn't part of our plan yet, especially before the wedding. I had mixed feelings, but I was mostly worried about how Gary would take the news. I thanked the doctor for her time, then slowly walked outside to my car, my mind racing.

I drove back to work and questioned whether I should call Gary immediately or wait until I got home. Anthony appeared at my desk, breaking me out of my contemplation, and asked how my appointment went. I simply danced around the question, saying everything was fine, but he seemed dubious. After he deposited a couple of files on my desk, he said, "If you get through this before noon, I'll take you out for lunch." I wasn't sure if I'd be able to do it, but I accepted the challenge and got to work.

Ten minutes before lunch, I dropped the folders on Anthony's desk, and I could tell he was impressed. He took me to a pizza place a block from the office, and as we sat, I tried to find out more details about him. He was defensive at first, then he began volunteering information, revealing that his father was a cold and insensitive man, but not mentioning anything about his mother or sister. I could sense that something was troubling him, but I decided not to push him further, so we discussed work and other inconsequential things before heading back to the office.

• • •

On my way home, I played out every possible scenario in my head about how I would break the news to Gary. I was so caught up in my thoughts that I took a wrong turn and went down a road I had never been on before. As I was about to turn around, I noticed a woman who looked like she had just fallen, sitting on the grass beside the sidewalk, so I stopped the car and got out to help her.

"Are you okay?" I asked, approaching her. She was looking down at the ground, her face concealed. I took her arm and helped her up, and when she stood up, I was shocked to see that it was the same old lady with the walker from Gary's apartment—how was this possible?

"Hello again," she said ominously. "I'm Gaby."

I stared at her for a moment, trying to make sure that she was real. "We've met before, Gaby. Do you remember me?"

"Yes, of course, dear."

"I went back to the apartment and found out that you don't live there. Why do I keep seeing you? What do you want from me?"

"I have to go now, thank you for your help, dear," she replied, ignoring my questions.

She took a few steps forward, staring at my stomach, and said, "A girl."

"What?"

"You're having a baby girl," she replied casually.

"How do you know? Who are you? Please talk to me!"

She ignored me again and started hobbling down the sidewalk. Her body seemed to disappear slowly as she got further away, but I couldn't let her leave again without getting any answers, so I yelled down the street at her, hoping she would hear me. "Gaby, wait! You can't leave me like this!" I was distracted by a car that roared down the road beside us, and when I looked back, she was gone. I couldn't have been more confused. Would Gary believe this if I told him?

• • •

When I got home, the overwhelming smell of roast beef turned my stomach. Gary heard me at the front door and came to greet me.

"What happened to you? I was worried sick!" he asked.

"Why?"

"Why? Because it's eight o'clock, Ellen, and you're usually home by five! Where have you been?" he asked, his worry translating as anger.

"I'm sorry, baby. I took a wrong turn and stopped for five minutes to help a woman who had fallen on the side of the road. I didn't realise I was gone for that long."

He wrapped his arms around me and told me that he loved me. Sometimes I wondered what I did to deserve such a wonderful man. I took off my shoes and put down my bag before walking to the bedroom to change my clothes. He followed me in, able to tell that I wasn't acting like myself.

"What's going on? Is there something you're not telling me?"

I wanted this conversation to end so badly.

"Everything is fine, baby, we can talk about it later. Let's eat, I'm starving," I lied.

We walked to the kitchen together and sat down to eat. Gary opened a bottle of wine and leaned over to pour me a glass. "None for me, thanks," I said, pulling the glass away.

"No wine? Are you sick? What did the doctor say today?" he asked, looking worried.

"Well… one of the things she said is that wine is not recommended for pregnant women," I said timidly, glancing over at him to see what his reaction would be.

"Wait! Are you saying what I think you're saying?"

"I am! You're going to be a father!" I answered, smiling back at him and eagerly anticipating his response.

He laughed and cried at the same time, leaping out of his chair so fast that it flipped over onto the floor. He raced over to me and pulled me out of my chair and hugged me so tightly that it took my breath away. I was relieved that he was so happy.

"When are we due?" he said, trying to calm down.

"December! We're having a Christmas baby!"

As I said this, I began to feel sad, remembering that Vicki was supposed to have a baby around Christmas before she miscarried— it wasn't fair, and it made me nervous to tell her the news. Gary and I immediately started making arrangements, and decided that we should get married in June, because I would be six months along if we kept the date we'd originally planned for.

Before I went to bed, I wrote six words in my diary:

I am having a baby girl!

CHAPTER EIGHTEEN

HEARTBREAK

Even though I hadn't told anyone, I think most people in the office knew I was pregnant because my baby bump started showing, and it was becoming more difficult to hide. I decided it was time to formally tell my boss, and when I did, he seemed happy for me, though I could sense that he thought it might be difficult to replace me when I go on maternity leave. I felt guilty that my coworkers knew my big news before I even told my father, or Vicki for that matter. She would be mad at me for not telling her a few weeks ago, but I wanted to wait until I passed the first critical stage so I didn't jinx it. She and Robert were coming over for dinner that night, so I planned on making the announcement then.

I decided to tell my father first, so I left work a few minutes early and drove to his house. When I got there, his car was in the driveway, but he didn't answer when I rang the doorbell. I walked around to the back of the house, but it was also empty and the door to the backyard was locked. I peeped through the kitchen window and noticed a plate sitting on the table, and it looked as though the food on it hadn't been touched. I thought he might be upstairs, so I rang the doorbell again and again, with no answer.

I riffled through my purse to see if I had the house key, but for some reason it was nowhere to be found. Growing more worried, I walked over to Rita's house, thinking that he might be there or she might know where he was. Thankfully, she answered the door, but then she informed me that she hadn't seen him for a few days. "Usually he calls me or comes over for coffee. I didn't want to bother him, I know he needs time alone every once in a while. You don't think something is wrong, do you?" she asked, looking worried.

I drove home to get the key, and when I got there, Gary was preparing dinner. He saw that I was overcome with worry and decided to come back to my father's house with me. When we got there, I unlocked the door, and as we entered, we heard music blaring throughout the house. "Dad? Dad, are you here?" I yelled, as I walked over to the radio and shut it off. I looked in the living room and the dining room, but he was nowhere to be found. We thought that perhaps he was sleeping, so Gary went to check his bedroom while I stayed downstairs to look in the other rooms. When I got to the kitchen, I heard Gary let out an earth-shattering scream, and I raced to the bottom of the stairs.

"John, John are you okay? Ellen, call an ambulance!" Gary shouted from upstairs.

"Oh my God! What's wrong, Gary? Is my Dad okay?" I yelled back.

"Hurry! Call an ambulance, Ellen. He's lying on the floor and is non-responsive!"

I began panicking, my hands shaking so badly that I had a hard time dialing 9-1-1. The operator answered and assured me that the ambulance would be there shortly, and then I rushed upstairs to the bedroom and saw my father lying on the floor, while Gary tried to perform CPR. I dropped to my knees next to him and checked for a pulse, but I couldn't feel anything. Five minutes later, the ambulance arrived—it felt like an eternity—and the paramedics assessed his condition and said that it was too late and there was nothing they could do. His body was ice cold, he must have been there for a few hours already. We watched them put his body into an ambulance and take him away, as I crumbled to the ground, crying my heart out, while Gary tried unsuccessfully to console me. We followed the ambulance to the hospital, where the doctor confirmed his death. "We're going to perform an autopsy, with your permission of course. It looks like he had heart attack, but we need to confirm it," the doctor said.

I told Catherine first, barely able to get the words out, and she said that she would call the others. Luckily, Daniel was staying in town with James, and Beth was with Catherine. They arrived at the hospital thirty minutes later, and we all gathered in the emergency room and stood around my father's bed, our hearts were broken. "He's with Mom now," Catherine said, trying to comfort us, before I excused myself and went to get some air.

I called Vicki from the hospital and told her what happened, going through all the details of that horrific day, my words filled with regret that I wasn't there when he needed me the most. When I was done, I let it slip that I was pregnant—I don't know why I chose that moment to tell her. My emotions were running high and I couldn't keep it in any longer. Vicki was devastated about my father and she told me that this was a sign—when one life ends, another begins, and every time I look at my child, I will see my beloved father.

• • •

Catherine took care of the funeral arrangements with James and, on the day of the funeral, I wore a black wrap-around dress to hide my baby bump, hoping that my siblings wouldn't be able to tell. At the funeral home, I leaned over my father's casket, my heart dropping when I saw him, and whispered, "Dad, I hope you find Mom in heaven. Please tell her that I miss her and love her, and I love you." Then, I put my mouth closer to his ear. "You're going to be grandparents, I'm pregnant with a baby girl, Dad," I whispered, touching his face as tears rushed down mine.

After the funeral home, we went to the church and were greeted by family and friends. I stood on the podium to deliver the eulogy, unable to control my emotions. "I can't do this, James," I stuttered, looking at my brother, who was standing next to me. "It's okay, Ellen. I'll do it," he responded, clinging onto my hand. He delivered a heartfelt eulogy, which we had written together, and we all said goodbye to my father.

At the cemetery, I placed two red roses on my mother and father's tombstone, both of their names etched onto it, now reunited forever. Then, I walked over to Anna's grave, laying down a pink rose for her and a red one for her mother. Overwhelmed, I sat on the ground to talk to Anna and the speckled butterfly landed on my shoulder. "I'm pregnant, Anna, but I'm sure you knew that already," I said, smiling up at the sky. I felt a hand caressing the side of my face, and heard a faint voice say, "It's a girl." I turned to look, but no one was there, except for Gary, who was waiting for me back on the path.

When we left the cemetery, my brothers and sisters came to my house, along with Vicki and Robert. We talked about what we would do with our family home, and Catherine said she would move in and pay for its upkeep. This made me immensely happy, there were so many memories within the four walls of that house.

"Gary and I have news to share," I said hesitantly—when would we all be together again like this again?—as I looked over at my fiancé for some backup.

Everyone stared at us eagerly, Vicki grinning from ear to ear because she already knew what we were about to reveal.

The cat came running out of the bedroom and jumped on me.

"You got a cat!" Beth screeched, as she tried to pick him up.

"Is that your big news?" added Catherine.

Gary and I look at each other, and then yelled, "We're pregnant!" in unison.

"We're due this Christmas!" he continued, with proud eyes.

The mood immediately shifted from despair and heartbreak to joy and excitement, and I could feel my parents' happiness embracing all of us. The baby became the focus of our conversation for the rest of the afternoon, and when everyone left, I went straight to bed, ready for the day to be over.

In the middle of the night, I got up to get a glass of water and, as I tried to find my way to the kitchen in the dark, I came across Patch standing in the middle of the hallway, staring at a dark silhouette on the ceiling, with his body in an erect position and his tail moving rapidly from side to side as if he were ready to attack something. I walked slowly towards him, trying to see what the shadow was, but as I did, he leapt into the air towards me. I let out a piercing shriek, and Gary came running out of the bedroom. "What's going on, Ellen?" he asked. After I told him what happened, he said that there was nothing there—as he always did—and we went back to bed, closing the door behind us.

• • •

The next day, after Gary left for work, I went to my car and took another look in the trunk, hoping to find the Ouija board, but it wasn't there. I thought I was losing my mind, and I desperately wanted to solve this mystery. I concluded that the only person who might be able to help me was Carmine—the psychic I visited a few years ago—so I booked an appointment for that day. When I left the house, I told Gary that I made plans to go out for dinner after work with a couple of my colleagues, and that he shouldn't expect me home until later that evening. I hated lying to him, but I had no choice, he wouldn't approve of me doing this. He once told me that psychics can mess with people's heads and that it was always better to consult a professional, but I desperately needed answers.

As I thought about everything that had happened, I realized that the number seven seemed to appear everywhere—Anna and I were both seven years old when she died; she was born on the seventh day of the seventh month; her house number was seventy-seven; the little boy in my dream was seven and the hallway he led me down had seven doors. I was overwhelmed and confused by this number as it constantly swirled around in my head, and I became determined to finally understand what it meant.

• • •

After work, I drove to Carmine's house, and when I walked up the driveway and rang the doorbell, I felt a prickly sensation creeping down the back of my neck. She opened the door, still looking the same as she had before, with her trendy clothes and perfectly styled hair, and she immediately led me to the little room downstairs. She could tell that I was nervous, so she tried to make me feel relaxed and ease me into the session. "Take a deep breath, Ellen. Open your mind and release your negative energy. You're safe here, just relax," she said in a calming tone. I sat at the table, staring down at the flickering candles that were placed in the middle, and she leaned forward to lay her hands over mine—they were burning hot. She looked me straight in the eye and started talking.

"I see four spirits around you, Ellen."

"Four? Are my parents here?"

"No, I don't feel them," she answered. "I see a young girl, a young woman, and an old woman. I'm sensing positive energy from them. They are good spirits."

"And the fourth one?"

"It's something dark… very dark indeed—" she paused. "It's something evil, and it feeds off your energy, like a parasite. This malevolent spirit enjoys scaring you and creating chaos around you."

I sat completely still, cold terror enveloping my entire body. "But I don't understand. What does this evil spirit want from me? Why has it latched itself onto me?" I mumbled, perhaps trying to conceal my fear from the demon, as it lingered in the corner, waiting to pounce.

"As I told you, when you visited me last, your ability to talk to the dead attracts all kinds of spirits. Ellen, have you ever used a Ouija board before?"

I felt sick and began to hyperventilate. "A few times… I had one but—"

"You had or you have?" she interrupted.

I explained how it disappeared from my trunk and that I was unable to find it since then.

"And you're sure no one removed it from your trunk?" she

replied, looking deeply concerned about the information I had just given her.

"Yes, I'm definitely sure about that."

"Hmm... very interesting. When you finished using it last, did you say, 'Goodbye Ouija' before closing it?"

"I can't remember, but I'm sure I did."

"Have you ever seen this dark entity before?"

"Yes, a few times. One time it strangled me in my room, and another time it grabbed my arm and tried to pull me into my trunk."

"And what were you doing when that happened?"

"Well... when it grabbed my arm, I was looking for the Ouija board in my car—"

"Okay, listen to me, Ellen," she interrupted, looking panicked. "You need to get rid of it as soon as you find it. The last time you were here, I told you to burn some sage in your house. Did you do that?" I nodded, and she continued. "You should also get some holy water and splash it on every corner of your house."

"Well... I burned the sage before, and that obviously didn't work, so—"

"Do it again, please trust me. Don't give it the time or space, Ellen. You need to tell yourself that you aren't afraid of it... convince yourself that it doesn't exist. No matter what you do, don't let it in."

As she said those words, the lights flickered and went off, and the candles all went out at once. We heard a loud bang from the hallway, and then the door slammed shut. Then, we heard the voice of a woman, screaming, "Leave her alone!" and another deep voice that sounded demonic, yelling, "You will burn in hell!" before it started hissing and panting. Carmine tried to keep calm, but I could tell she was alarmed, and then she stared blankly in front of her and began screaming, "My back, my back it burns... get some water, WATER, please!" I plucked the glass of water off the table and ran around behind her to splash it on her, as she shrieked in agony. When the voices stopped, the lights turned back on and the candles lit on their own.

"What in the hell was that?" I yelled, scared to death.

Carmine was still in shock.

"This has never happened here before, Ellen. I think you need to see a specialist. I don't think I can help you anymore," she said, her voice trembling in fear.

"Let me see your back," I demanded, as I pulled her shirt up. There were seven red dots the size of dimes lined up vertically along her spine.

"It burns, can you see anything?"

"It looks okay, just a few red marks," I lied, hoping that she wouldn't blame me for this.

I wanted to run, worried sick about how all this might impact my baby. I put a twenty-dollar bill on the table and left, and when I got to my car, I noticed some letters traced in the dust on the trunk. As I got closer, they became clearer—it read "Zozo." I jumped back a few feet, my purse dropping to the ground and my heart beating out of my chest. After a moment, I got up the courage to open the trunk and couldn't believe my eyes—the Ouija board was lying open inside, as if it had never moved. I slammed the trunk shut and drove until I found a garbage container on the side of the road, and then I parked and threw the board in.

Now the demon would stop hunting me, right?

When I pulled into my driveway, I saw Gary sitting on the porch, looking out of his mind with worry because it was almost midnight. At first, I thought he was mad, but when I saw him smile it made me feel better. He helped me out of the car, and then I told him that I had to drive a colleague home and she ended up living farther than I expected. We went to bed and talked for a while about our wedding that Saturday, as I concealed my terror about what happened that night.

CHAPTER NINETEEN
WEDDING BELLS

The cloudless sky and warm sun couldn't have been more perfect for our wedding day. I felt at my best, especially because my dress still fit me. I put on some makeup and curled my hair in loose waves, before Robert and Vicki picked me up and drove me to the church in a red convertible they had rented. When I arrived at the church, James and Catherine waited for me outside, and Daniel and Beth were already inside with a few other guests. I took a deep breath, inhaling the sweet fragrance that escaped from my floral bouquet as James walked me down the aisle. The church pews were decorated with white ribbons and bows, adding a romantic charm to the ambiance. When I saw Gary at the altar, looking tall and handsome in his black tuxedo, I fell in love all over again.

He took my hands and we stared into each other's eyes—I was certain that this would last forever. Our priest was the same one I remember from when I was a child, and his presence made me feel connected to my mother. He read some verses from the Bible about the sanctity of marriage and the unique and undying bond between man and wife, and then he asked us to exchange our vows. I untied the silky white ribbon around the piece of white parchment that I had written my vows on, and then slowly read through each one. I told Gary that he was the one person that I could always count on, and I promised to support him and be there for him no matter what trials might arise in the future. I vowed that I would be true to him forever, and that I'd do anything it took to protect him and our child.

When I finished, he said the vows he had memorized, promising to protect me and ensure that I had the happiest life possible, and then he recited a beautiful rendition of his favourite poem. Next, the priest delivered the wedding blessings, as we said, "I do" to one another and exchanged our rings. "I love you so much, sweetheart," Gary whispered in my ear, as the priest declared us man and wife. "I love you more," I replied, standing on my tip-toes to kiss him.

We walked down the aisle hand in hand to the beautiful sounds of the church organ and wedding bells. When we got outside, our photographer signaled everyone to gather to take a photo, and in one click, this day became immortalized. We moved to a beautiful, green park beside the church, and stood under a tall, purple lilac tree. I looked over and saw the butterfly resting on my shoulder, always a constant companion. I could feel Anna there with me, and was overjoyed that she was a part of this special day.

After we finished taking photos, we gathered in the basement of the church for a lunch buffet, where Vicki and Beth had elaborately decorated the room with flowers, crystals, and candles. I had never felt so happy and I thanked my lucky stars that I found someone like Gary—I don't know what I would have become without him.

It was beautiful and bright when we left, twilight filling the air with deep orange and purple hues. We arrived home at seven o'clock, and went upstairs to the baby's room, which we had painted and decorated the week before—this was so much better than a honeymoon. We changed into comfortable clothes and went outside to sit in the backyard, drinking tea while Gary rubbed my stomach. "We need to think of some baby names," he said. I felt myself tense up.

"How about Johnathan?" he suggested.

"What if it's a girl?" I asked, already knowing that it would be.

"In that case, I think I know what name you would pick."

"You do?"

"I think we should call her Anna. I know how much that name means to you."

He knew me so well.

"Thank you! I love you so much, baby."

"I love you more!"

The sparkly moon shone on the garden, bouncing off the ornaments like a light show. I wanted to savour that moment for as long as possible before bedtime. Sometimes life is kind and sends us a bit of magic dust to remind us how lucky we are.

That day, I felt like the luckiest girl in the world.

• • •

Two weeks after the wedding, we received our photo album and eagerly waited for Vicki and Robert to come over for dinner so we could look at it. Gary cooked us steaks, grilled vegetables, and roasted potatoes on the barbecue, and we ate together on the patio. As we flipped through the photos, we were in awe of how beautifully they turned out—except for one, which the photographer had warned me about. He placed it in an envelope and slid it in the plastic pocket at the back of the album. I hadn't opened it yet, and I tried to hide it, but Vicki saw me fidgeting.

"Are there more photos?" Vicki asked, reaching over to take it from me.

"Not sure. It's probably just the negatives or something," I lied.

"Well you should open it. Aren't you curious?

"Not now, I'll open it later."

"Just open it, sweetie," Gary said, trying to avoid making the situation more awkward.

I felt pressured and decided to open the envelope against my better judgement. Inside the envelope, I found a note that read:

Ellen,

I hesitated before giving you this photo, but I thought you might want to see it. There's something strange about it, and I personally can't explain it, but maybe you'll know what it is.

A chill ran down my spine—what could possibly be so bad about this photo that he would be scared to show me? "What is it?" Gary asked, interrupting my train of thought. "It's just another copy of one of the photos in the album," I lied, confirming my decision not to look at it until I was alone. I stuffed the note back in the envelope and went to the bedroom to store it in my night table.

"Let's talk about something else," Gary said, when I got back to the living room.

"Yeah, let's talk about baby names!" Vicki said.

"Have you guys decided on any yet?" Robert asked.

"Anna," I said, without thinking.

"Wow, you say that as if you already know it's a girl! Is it?" Vicki asked.

"No, I mean… I don't know."

Gary winked at me, "I think she's secretly wishing for a girl."

Vicki talked about the challenges of the adoption process and how it seemed like it would be impossible for them. They had hoped to adopt within a year when they applied internationally, but it turned out to be just as complicated, and I could tell that they were starting to lose hope.

"I know it's not the same, but you'll be an aunt soon," I said, thinking that this might make her feel at least a bit better.

"And you can spoil him or her as much as you want," Gary added.

"Be prepared, I'm going to spoil this baby!" Vicki said, a huge smile spreading across her face.

After they left, I rushed to the bedroom to retrieve the picture from my night table, and Gary followed me, curious about what I was hiding. I sat on the corner of the bed, pulling out the 5x7 photo from the envelope. In the picture, Gary stood on the left, Robert and Vicki in the middle, and I was on the right, happily smiling into the lens. Beside me, there were four shadows, two women and a girl along with a smoky black fog that seemed to hover above my head. I couldn't believe what I was seeing and, frightened to death, I threw it onto the floor in front of me. As soon as it landed, it caught on fire, and we both let out bellowing screams, before Gary poured his glass of water on it to put it out.

"Oh my God, Ellen, what the hell just happened?" he yelled.

"I don't know what's going on! I can't explain any of this," I cried. "Why are all these weird things happening to me?"

For the first time, Gary looked genuinely afraid. I had never seen him that way and thought that perhaps now he would believe everything I had told him.

"Well… there's nothing we can do. Maybe we should call an exorcist!" he said jokingly.

"Gary, this isn't a joke! Why can't you take this seriously for once?" I answered, growing impatient and angry.

"I'm just trying to help, Ellen. I don't know what to say."

I told him what happened at the psychic and about the Ouija board, and also that I had cleansed our house with sage, as Carmine suggested. "I don't know what else to do," I wept, feeling hopeless. He took a deep breath, trying to make sense of it all. "Maybe that's why the cat is acting so weird. He can probably sense those spirits around you. Animals have a sixth sense, you know," he said, his eyes revealing his concern. We were both exhausted and agreed to discuss this more in the morning. Gary put Patch in the basement and closed the door, and before I went to bed, I wrote four words in my diary:

Please make it stop!

CHAPTER TWENTY
GHOST FROM THE PAST

Summer came to an end, and fall swiftly brought in cool air and covered the trees in beautiful red and gold leaves. On a crisp Thursday evening in September, I put on my warm sweater and suede boots to go for a walk in the park with Gary. We walked in silence, which I didn't mind, and enjoyed the fragrance of the leaves and the crackling sounds they made as we trampled upon them. I began to think about all the inexplicable things that I had seen over the last few months, but I tried to free my mind from my fear and make happier memories with my wonderful husband. Those spirits belonged in the past, I had to forget about them and leave them there.

We stopped at a bench to sit and drink the hot cocoa that Gary made for us. "Your birthday is coming up," he said, breaking the silence. "How about we go out for dinner at your favourite French restaurant?" I couldn't believe I was turning twenty-seven already, it seemed like it was only yesterday that I was seven years old, playing with Anna in her backyard and chasing butterflies. "That sounds like a great plan!" I answered. He wrapped his arms around me and we continued to walk, hand in hand.

• • •

On my birthday, I took a warm bath and went to the living room to read. Before I sat down, I opened the side table drawer, where I stored all my magazines. A few unopened letters, which I must have picked up from the mailbox a while ago and forgot to open, fell onto the floor. A small, blue envelope caught my eye, and when I looked closer, I saw Paul's name and return address written on the top left corner. I hesitated to open it, but curiosity got the better of me, so I ripped it open, my heart pounding in anticipation.

Dear Ellen,

Thank you for your letter, though I don't want you to think that you have to apologise to me. I completely understand why you left the restaurant so abruptly that day—I probably would've done the same thing, if the roles were reversed. But I want you to know that my love for you all those years ago was real, and I don't ever want you to doubt that. I hope that we can move on from this and be friends.

I am really happy now. I moved in with Sebastian and hope to spend the rest of my life with him. I love him so much. As you can imagine, my parents are no longer speaking to me, and even though it really hurts, I have come to accept it.

Please don't hate me.

Love,

Paul

My throat tightened—the last thing I wanted was for him to think that I hated him. I felt the urge to write him back, but what would be the use? Too much had happened between us, and I doubted that we could be friends after all this time. I walked to my bedroom and placed the letter in a souvenir box that I kept in the closet, and closed the door on Paul forever. It was time to come to terms with that part of my past. Even though it hurt that he kept this from me for so long, I admired his courage and was happy that he was finally being true to himself.

I slowly walked to the couch—my baby bump was growing bigger every day, and it was becoming more difficult to move around—and as soon as I sat down I felt a kick, which brought me back to my new reality, to my future. In just a few weeks, I was going to be a mother, and I was over the moon about it. I got up to change and get ready for dinner and eagerly waited for Gary to come home. When he walked in, I gave him a big hug and began to cry. "What's wrong, sweetie?" he asked, looking concerned. "Oh nothing, it must be hormones," I answered. I chose not to tell him about Paul's letter because I didn't want him to get mad, and in my mind that chapter of my life was over and belonged in the past. "Are you ready?" he asked, breaking me free from my thoughts. I picked up my jacket and purse. "I am now!" I answered, smiling at my future.

• • •

An hour later, we pulled in the restaurant's parking lot, and Gary helped me out of the car. Inside, the checkered floors and retro dining tables and chairs offered a romantic setting, and we sat at a small table for two, strategically placed in a private corner against the window. I browsed the menu and said to Gary, "You know I have to eat for two now, right?"

He laughed. "Go nuts, my love. It's your birthday, so eat anything you want!" I ordered French onion soup and their famous creamy Riesling chicken dish, and Gary got seafood soup and a center cut sirloin steak with frites. The waitress brought our appetizers first, and when she placed them on the table, the smell of the seafood turned my stomach. I rushed to the washroom and, when I regained my composure, I came back to the table and saw that Gary had thoughtfully sent the calamari platter back.

The waitress returned with our main courses, and I ate everything on my plate. "That's it, I'm officially a pig!" I said, taking in a deep breath. "Ah! Too full for dessert?" Never too full for dessert, I thought. We ordered cheesecake and coffee, I ate all of mine and half of Gary's, and we talked about what we should buy for the baby's room and how much things would change when we became parents. I could tell that something was troubling him, he seemed distracted and distant, but I didn't know why.

"What's going on, baby, you seem a bit off tonight," I asked.

"I'm sorry. Don't worry, everything is fine," he answered, as he fidgeted under the table. I decided not to push further.

"Okay good, what shall we do later? Do you want to—"

"Did you read the newspaper today?" he interrupted, staring down at the table.

"No... why? What's going on?"

"I hate to bring this up now, Ellen, but—" he paused. I could tell he was debating whether he should continue. "Jack, I mean Karl, was released from prison," he finished, reaching across the table to take my hand.

"Come again? What did you just say?" I answered, thinking I must have heard him incorrectly.

"He got out today, Ellen."

"And you decided to tell me this right now... on my birthday?"

"I'm so sorry, sweetie, I should have waited, but I didn't want you to think I was keeping anything from you."

So many thoughts raced through my head, and all of a sudden, I felt exposed and completely unsafe. "Gary, I want to go home right now. I don't want to be here anymore," I demanded.

He immediately asked for the bill, and I rushed out of the restaurant to the car. When he got in the other side, he started apologising repeatedly.

"How could he be out of prison already? He got seven years!"

"I know... the paper said that they let him out early for good behaviour."

I started wailing, partly from terror, but mostly because of rage. "How the hell could they let him out? What if he comes after us?"

"We can get a restraining order, sweetie," he said, trying to say anything to make the situation better.

"That's not going to stop him from coming after me, Gary," I snapped, knowing that this wasn't his fault, but unable to hold back my frustration.

When we got home, we went straight to bed. Gary held me tight all night, which made me feel safe. All this time I had been worried about the things that I couldn't see, when I should have been on guard against what was waiting for me right outside my door.

 • • •

When I got to work on Monday, I told Anthony about Jack being released from prison. I found myself constantly looking over my shoulder and checking my surroundings just in case he was there. He nearly killed that poor girl, what else was he capable of? Anthony was infuriated, and as soon as I finished my story, he started gathering information about how to file a restraining order.

"Don't worry, Ellen," he said as he looked up his friend, who was a criminal lawyer. "They put a bracelet on his ankle to monitor his whereabouts, so the police will know if he comes anywhere near you."

"I don't know if that would stop him from coming after me, though," I answered, remembering Jack's letter. He said that he'd always love me—would knowing I was married to Gary send him over the deep end?

"He's on parole, Ellen. One false move and he'll be thrown right back into prison."

"Sure, but by then it will be too late. Who knows what he could do?"

"Don't worry. I will call my friend and he will go to the court house to apply for a restraining order for you. Everything will be okay. What's most important now is that you don't kill yourself with worries, it's not good for you or the baby."

"Thank you for caring so much, it means a lot to me," I replied, feeling blessed that I had someone looking out for me.

 • • •

On my way home, I stopped at the salon and asked my hair dresser to cut my hair and dye it blonde. I wanted to be sure that, if Jack decided to come around, he would not be able to recognize me. When she was finished, I looked in the mirror, and I almost didn't recognize myself. My hair was five inches shorter, cut just below my chin, making my face look less round, and the blonde made my eyes sparkle.

When I got home and opened the front door, Gary came to greet me and, when he saw me, his mouth fell open. "Wow, you look—"

"Don't say anything," I answered, as I threw myself into his arms and sobbed. When I let go of him, I sat down on the chair in the entrance to take my shoes off. Patch sauntered towards us, but turned around and fled from the hallway as soon as he saw me.

"See, I told you. That stupid cat hates me."

"That's not true, sweetie, and by the way, I think your new look is super sexy," he answered, winking at me.

"I'm not going for sexy! Stop trying to make light of this awful situation," I retorted.

"I was just giving you a compliment… you're just a little emotional right now, Ellen," he answered, as he wiped the tears off my cheeks with the sleeve of his shirt. "But really, though, you look stunning. I like you as a blonde."

"Sure, but you have to say that," I smiled.

• • •

I was nervous about going to the office with my new haircut because I didn't know what my coworkers would think of it. When I walked in, everyone turned their heads to look at me, like I was a stranger.

"Oh my God! I almost didn't recognize you, Ellen," the receptionist said, as Anthony came walking to the front.

"Woah, Ellen, is that you?" he teased, with a surprised look on his face.

"Please don't laugh, Anthony."

"I'm not! You look… wait, is this a wig?"

"No silly!"

"Well, I like it, I really like it!"

He took me to his office and closed the door and told me that the restraining order took effect that day.

"Thank you so much for everything you've done for me, Anthony."

"Anytime, kiddo, I'm always here for you," he said as he handed me a business card.

"This is the information for a friend of mine. He's a cop and you can call him anytime."

"You're an angel, thank you!"

I let out a deep sigh of relief and started to feel safe again. Maybe I got all worked up for nothing, I thought.

* * *

After work, I stopped at Vicki's house to show off my new hair. "Wow! You look amazing!" she yelled as soon as she saw me. We went inside and sat in her kitchen, and I told her about Jack's release. She was devastated and worried for me, but also somewhat relieved that I was doing everything I could to protect myself.

"I'm so tired, Vicki. I can't deal with this shit anymore. I need to focus on the baby. She'll be here soon and will need my full attention," I said, resting my head in my hands.

"Ah! You just said she again!" she answered, trying to catch me.

"It's a bad habit. I don't really know if it's a boy or a girl."

She put her hands on her hips and raised her eyebrows.

"You can't fool me, Ellen Taylor. You know it's a girl and for some reason you just don't want to tell me!"

"Okay, fine. I'll tell you how I know, but you can't tell Robert or Gary," I said, as she nodded expectedly.

I told her the story about the old lady and how she revealed the gender of the baby to me.

"Good Lord, Ellen! Your life is like a freaky scary movie!"

She had no idea just how much.

* * *

After dinner that evening, Gary and I sat in the swing chair on the front porch. I had a strange feeling that we were being watched and, when I turned to look, I saw Patch staring at us through the window, his yellow eyes like two beacons of light shining on us.

"I think he's waiting for us to go to bed," Gary said, laughing.

"Okay, let's go, I have to be at the office early tomorrow anyway."

"I have to get up early too," he responded, taking my hand and leading me inside.

In the middle of the night, Gary started snoring and I couldn't sleep. I decided to go sleep on the couch, and as I slept, I dreamt about the house with the seven doors. I woke up, my heart pounding, and saw Patch beside my right leg, looking at me and growling. I pushed him off of me and went back to the bedroom, and when I shut the door, Gary woke up. "Are you okay, sweetie?" he asked, half asleep.

"Make love to me, baby," I whispered, desperate for him to be close to me. He took me in his arms and made love to me gently, like he was afraid to hurt me or the baby. That's just the kind of man he was, and I felt like I was blessed to have found him.

CHAPTER TWENTY-ONE
THE SEVENTH DOOR

The following Monday, I was the first one in the office, so I went to the kitchen to make myself a cup of coffee before trudging back to my desk to work on a huge pile of files that Anthony had left for me.

"Good morning. You're in early," Anthony said, popping his head around the corner.

"Oh my God, Anthony, you scared the shit out of me!"

"I'm sorry, Ellen, I didn't mean to startle you."

"It's okay. I guess I'm just a little jumpy these days."

"Let me make it up to you. I'll buy lunch today," he said as he walked away.

Even though I had a ton of work to do, I couldn't say no to him after everything he had done to keep Jack away from me, and I needed something to distract my anxious mind. When lunchtime came, Anthony took me to the pub next door, where they made the best burgers in town. Once we were done eating, he randomly asked if I had purchased a crib for the baby yet. I told him that I hadn't, but planned on going shopping that weekend. "If you're interested, I have one you might like," he said out of nowhere. He had never mentioned anything about having kids, or even a wife for that matter. He could tell that I was confused, so he added that his mother had kept his maple crib with a built-in changing table, as well as a seven-drawer dresser and a toy box. "It's good quality and in excellent condition. Looks like new," he said, trying to persuade me to take it.

"Wow. That's amazing. But what happens if you need it someday?"

"Nah, I'll never have kids. It's yours if you want it. Free of charge!"

"Why would you do that?" I asked, surprised by his immense generosity.

"Because you're my friend, and I like you."

"That's so nice of you, thank you. Would it be okay if I came to see it?"

"Of course, just say when and I'll take you. It's still at my family home—about an hour out of town—but it's a lovely drive and it will be worth the trouble. If you want, we could skip work and go tomorrow."

"If you say so, you're the boss!"

"Great, we'll leave early. Can you meet me at the office at seven thirty?"

"You bet. I'll be there!"

. . .

The next morning, I woke up with puffy eyelids and dark circles under my eyes because I didn't sleep enough. I wish I could stay home, I thought as I made a big cup of coffee. I couldn't stand Anthony up, especially because he was being so generous. "You're off to work awfully early, sweetie," said Gary, coming into the kitchen and pulling out a mug from the cupboard. I told him about the crib and that I was going to see it with Anthony that morning, and he looked disappointed that I didn't talk to him about it first. "I just want to see it, and then if it seems like we could use it, then we can go look at it together."

I fixed my hair, applied some lipstick and put on my black maternity jeans with an ivory blouse and cream-coloured jacket. When I pulled into the parking lot at the office, I saw Anthony waiting for me in his brand-new red Camaro. "Nice car!" I said, getting out of my old Toyota. "Fast car!" he replied with a proud smile. I noticed two coffees and a box of donuts in between the front seats when I got in. "Help yourself," he said.

I wasn't hungry, and my stomach was a little off, but I appreciated the coffee. I asked him if anyone would be waiting for us at his family's house and he said no—he paid someone to come by and fix up the yard and check on it every once in a while, but no one lived there. I had a million other questions to ask him, but I kept quiet. He noticed the necklace with a heart pendent dangling around my neck.

"Is that new?"

"Gary gave it to me for my birthday."

"Shoot, I forgot it was your birthday! Why didn't you remind me?"

"Don't worry about it."

I rubbed his arm to reassure him.

"I'll make it up to you," he promised.

"Don't worry about it! It's just a birthday. You can get me something next year!"

He turned up the music, and we rolled down the windows to feel the warm air, which was unusual for this time in October. As we got closer to the house, my anxiety heightened, and I started getting restless, shifting around in my seat and twisting my hair into small spirals—I always did that when something bothered me.

"Are you okay?" Anthony asked, seeing that I wasn't acting like myself.

"Yes, I just have a strange feeling. I'm not sure why," I said, as we got closer to his house.

"What sort of strange feeling?"

"I feel like I've been here before, but it's weird because I've never been to this neighbourhood."

"Maybe you came here when you were younger or something. Don't worry so much, Ellen! Are you sure you're okay?" he asked as we pulled up to his house.

The ranch style home was a perfect reflection of the fifties era, with its single-level floorplan and a two-tiered wooden fence that surrounded the property. Its exterior showed its age, but I could tell that someone put in a lot of effort to maintain it. We pulled into the driveway and walked up the stairs of the porch, and Anthony put the key in the door and walked in first, while I stayed outside. "Come in, Ellen," he urged. "Nothing's going to bite you!" The second I stepped inside, my heart started pounding. I knew that I had been in this house before and I had an overwhelming feeling that we weren't alone. I told him that I needed to use the bathroom, and he took my hand and walked me down the long and narrow hallway—I counted seven doors, all of them closed. I used the bathroom, while he waited outside the door. When I came out, I asked him to show me around, and just like that, it all made sense.

"Oh my God! This is the house!" I shrieked, my voice trembling.

"What are you talking about, Ellen?" he asked, his eyebrows raised in confusion.

"You're the little boy in my dream, aren't you?"

"Your dream? What dream? You're freaking me out right now. Can you tell me what the hell is going on?"

The hair on the back of my neck stood up, as he opened and closed each door, one by one, and just like in my dream, he couldn't open the seventh one. I was shaking so much that I felt like I was going to faint. When I asked him why the last door was locked, he said that his parents used it for storage for their valuables and they wanted to make sure that no one could get inside.

"Why are you so freaked out about this, Ellen?"

"Can you please unlock that door?" I answered, pointing to it and ignoring his question.

"Of course, that's where the crib is."

"Do you have the key?"

"Yes. You're really acting weird. What's going on?"

"Just open the damn door please!"

"Okay, calm down," he said, taking the key out of his pocket.

As he put the key into the lock, I was half-expecting that I would wake up from yet another dream. I never thought that I would ever find out what was behind that door, and now that I was so close, I was unsure if I really wanted to know. I couldn't believe that this twenty-year mystery was coming to an end—or was it just the beginning?

Anthony opened the door, and we were instantly hit by a cold breeze and an overwhelming scent of flowers that took my breath away. In a way, I felt like Alice, when she falls down the rabbit hole before going to Wonderland. I looked around the room in disbelief. There was a white dresser in between two single beds, and on it rested a hairbrush and a hand mirror. The baby furniture leaned against the far-right wall. My eyes locked in on a red firetruck that sat on top of a large toy box—it was an exact replica of the one my little brother Daniel had when we were kids. It seemed like no one had used the room in years, this was all too surreal to me. Anthony leaned against the door frame, watching me, confused by my reaction, and then the lights flickered.

"Anthony, what's happening?"

"I don't know. Maybe something is wrong with the power?"

"I feel like a spirit is in here with us," I said, looking around the room.

"You're creeping me out, Ellen. Can you see anything?"

As soon as he asked this, I saw a figure of a woman sitting on one of the beds, staring at me with a blank look on her face. She had short, dark red hair, white satin skin, and hazel brown eyes.

"I see a woman. She's right there," I said, pointing to her and telling him more about her appearance.

"Oh my God, Ellen, you're describing my mother, Alma. But that makes no sense… she died many years ago."

"She's here, Anthony. I can see her, she's sitting on the bed. She says she has a message for you."

I was as scared as he was, but I tried to keep calm—after all, I had seen ghosts many times before, and she didn't seem as threatening as the demon who always tried attacking me. As I looked closer, I began to recognize her. She was the same figure who was always with Anna, but I couldn't figure out how she was connected to Anthony. As these thoughts swirled about in my mind, I felt a pressure on my chest that was so heavy that I found it hard to breathe. The next thing I knew, everything was fuzzy and my body went limp, it was almost as if the woman's spirit took over, and then I blacked out. As I regained consciousness, I felt like I hadn't slept in days and I couldn't remember any details about what had just happened. Then, when I looked around the room again, I saw Anthony crying on his knees.

I knelt on the floor beside him and asked him to explain what happened. "You… you became my mother and you spoke to me with her voice!" he said, his entire body convulsing. Then he told me that, as she spoke, he sat in front of what appeared to be his mother, and she held his hand. She said that she had been wanting to tell him how sorry she was to have left him behind at such a young age—he was only seven years old when she died—but living became unbearable, so she swallowed a bottle of pills and decided to take her fate into her own hands. She also told him that she felt guilty for leaving him behind with his father and that he didn't deserve to be treated so poorly by him. Finally, he placed his head on her shoulder and cried, while she stroked his hair softly. "And the next thing I knew, she was gone, and you were sitting on the bed!" he finished. My head was spinning, and I held onto Anthony, as we cried in each other's arms.

Speechless, he took my hand, and we walked out of the bedroom as he closed the door behind us, forgetting to lock it. We got to the living room and he poured himself a glass of whisky and offered me some water, then he removed the plastic cover from the couch so we could sit and talk more. "I'm so sorry, Anthony, what just happened was out of my control," I said, then continued to tell him about my recurring dream of this house ever since Anna died when I was seven. I explained how she died, and described the woman that I had seen with her for all these years.

"When did your mother die, Anthony?"

"September of 1967," he replied.

"What day in September?"

"The seventeenth, why?"

I choked on my drink and nearly dropped my glass.

"You won't believe this, but that is the exact same day that Anna died!" I shrieked.

"Are you kidding me?"

"No, I'm not. This is way too weird! Do you think that their deaths are connected somehow?" I asked.

"I think they might be. If they both died tragically at the same time, then maybe their souls are linked," he answered, before he began telling me about the day his mother committed suicide, and he revealed a secret that he had been hiding for years—that he felt responsible for it.

"On the day she died, my father forced me to go to the grocery store, even though my mother begged me to stay with her. When we returned, I searched the whole house for my mother, opening each door one by one. Her bedroom door was locked, so I found the key, and when I got inside—" he paused, his voice trembling from the pain of remembering that horrific day. "When I got inside, I saw my mother lying on her bed, lifeless and as white as a ghost. My father rushed in and demanded that I go to the basement, and I waited there for what seemed like an eternity until I heard the ambulance's sirens. I could hear a bunch of people moving around upstairs, and then it was completely quiet. I never saw her again because my father wouldn't let me go to the funeral and was unwilling to explain how she died. Instead, he sent me to a psychologist so that he wouldn't have to talk to me about it. She helped me a lot, and she even had a son who was the same age as me... I think his name was Robert. My father died from cancer a few years later, and I inherited the house. I didn't have the heart to sell it. I feel like she's still here, sleeping in her bed."

"I'm so sorry that happened, Anthony. That must have been so hard," I responded, at a loss for words. I remembered Robert telling Vicki and me about his mom and how she helped a young boy cope with the loss of his mother. All the people I knew and the strange events that kept occurring seemed to be connected, and it was far beyond a mere coincidence.

"What about your sister? Where was she when all this happened?" I asked, trying to put more pieces of the puzzle together.

"Jane moved to Chicago when she was nineteen years old, and I haven't seen her since," he answered, his face full of regret and sadness.

I held his hand tightly and told him again that this wasn't his fault. As I stared into his eyes, I felt our undeniable connection—we were like two lost souls who had finally found one another, and I was sure that we did for a reason.

Then, as I thought about everything, it all started to make sense. Anthony's mother passed away on the same day as Anna, and somehow, they connected with one another in the afterlife. I had seen this woman so many times, and in a way, she had become one of my protectors. I suddenly realized that meeting Anthony was no coincidence—Alma somehow arranged for me to meet him. She knew that I could see her and that eventually I would be able to help her give her son the message that she was sorry for leaving him behind and that she loved him. All this time I was afraid of her, and never knew why she kept appearing to me, when all she wanted to do was be close to her son again.

"How can I ever thank you enough for this, Ellen?" he said, breaking my train of thought. His despair was now replaced by joy and hope, and in that moment, I knew his mother's mission had been fulfilled.

"Don't thank me, Anthony, this is destiny. We both needed this. Your mother loved you, and now you don't have to feel guilty about her death anymore."

We sat in silence for a few minutes. "Are you still interested in the furniture?" he said, smiling and trying to lighten the mood.

"Of course! I'd like to buy it from you."

"I said it before and I'll say it again, kiddo, it's yours. Consider it a gift from my mother. I'll even have it delivered to your house!"

I had to take it, his mother would have wanted me to. I felt it in my heart.

CHAPTER TWENTY-TWO
GOODBYE BUTTERFLIES

Dreams do mean something, I had proof of that now. It took years before they manifested in real life, but now I felt enlightened after having been kept in the dark for so long. The thought of not knowing the meaning of my other dreams scared me, and even though I threw out my Ouija board, it didn't mean that Zozo was gone for good.

As my due date drew closer, Gary and I scrambled to get the baby's room ready and buy everything we might need. Anthony delivered the furniture at the end of October, and we mounted a pink mobile with dangling angels and stars above it. Everything was perfect, and I couldn't wait to welcome our baby to our home. As we sat in the nursery, I was filled with doubt, "What if it's a boy?" I said.

Gary laughed and looked amused. "No problem, we'll just repaint the room blue and change a few things," he answered nonchalantly. I suppose I had no reason to think that it wouldn't be a girl. After all, Gaby and Anna told me so.

• • •

On the last Saturday in November, Vicki and Robert picked us up to go out for dinner. When we arrived at our favourite Mexican restaurant, we ordered tapas platters, and I ate so much that I thought my stomach was going to pop. "I feel like a beached whale, and I probably look like one!" I said, hoping that I wouldn't break the chair as I shifted to get up to go to the restroom. "You look beautiful! You're having a baby in four weeks, it's totally normal to feel uncomfortable," Vicki assured me. On the way back to the table, I glanced over to the front door of the restaurant, and my heart stopped as I saw a man who looked just like Jack. When I got back to the table, I looked again, but he was gone. I shook myself out of my paranoia and settled back into my seat, while Vicki gave me an inquisitive look, knowing that I was worried about something. I brushed it off and tried to push it out of my mind and enjoy the evening.

. . .

Later that night, as I slept soundly, I was jolted awake by a strange noise. I looked around the room, but nothing was there. I thought it might just be the cat, up to no good in the living room, so I tiptoed out of the bedroom and closed the door slowly behind me so I didn't wake up Gary. As I walked down the dark hallway, I saw Patch, his back to me, crouching with his tail tucked behind his body, his ears perked up as if he was listening to something. He stared down the hallway at the kitchen entrance, and when I passed him, he got scared and let out an agonizing meow. I walked towards the kitchen to see what he was looking at, and I froze when I saw Anna and Anthony's mother, Alma, sitting at the kitchen table, their eyes flickering like bright lights in the dark.

"Anna? Why are you here? Why is Alma with you?" I asked as I started crying. Anna's ghost had never seemed so real before, and suddenly I was transported back to a time when we were both young and carefree.

"She's my guardian angel, Ellen," she whispered.

"We're here to warn you," Alma said.

"Warn me about what?" I asked, shaking my head.

"You need to be careful, Ellen, very careful," Alma answered.

Before I could say anything else, they disappeared. I pulled a chair out and sat at the table, as Patch jumped onto my lap and purred—he had never done that before. It's was almost like he felt sorry for me and wanted to comfort me. I turned my head towards the patio and saw two roses placed against the outside of the door, one white and one blue. I slid it open and picked them up, their petals soft and slightly warm, and put them in a glass vase before going back to bed, as Patch eagerly followed behind me.

. . .

The backyard looked picturesque, suited for a Christmas postcard. Gary and I sat in front of the fireplace, drinking coffee and listening to the calming sounds of the crackling wood. I started to tidy up the house, while Gary went outside to shovel the snow that was taking over our driveway. An hour later, I heard him come through the door and ran to his side, pulling him in for a kiss.

"Wow, what did I do to deserve that?" he asked, as he rubbed my belly to feel the baby kick.

"I love you, that's all! What do you want to do today?" I asked.

"Oh, I know! Let's put up the Christmas tree!"

"Isn't it a bit early?"

"I don't think so, it's December! Besides, what if the baby decides to arrive earlier?"

He agreed and then went to the basement to get the tree, and we put it up in the corner of the family room next to the window. We decorated it with strings of white lights and colourful ornaments— it looked perfectly imperfect! It didn't take long for the cat to charge into the tree and knock down a few decorations. "Well, that was to be expected, wasn't it?" I said, as Patch played with a fallen ornament on the floor. As we watched him and laughed, the doorbell rang. "Must be the pizza guy," Gary said, as I walked to the front of the house to open it.

I undid the lock, and then swung the door open, saying, "Yay, pizza! We've been—"

"Ellen?"

My heart stopped and my limbs went cold as I stared at Jack on the other side of the door. He looked exactly the same, except maybe a bit older, and dressed in our local pizza place's uniform.

"Jack... I mean Karl—whatever your name is—what the *hell* are you doing here?"

"Well, I have to work as a condition of my parole, so I got a job at... wow you changed your hair... and you're pregnant!"

"I heard you got out of prison. I didn't think you would have the guts to come back to the same neighbourhood."

"It's the only home I know, Ellen. I have nowhere else to go and—"

"Yes, you do. You belong in prison! You need to get the fuck out of my house right now!"

"I'm happy to see you're doing well," he said, handing me our pizza. "I'd like it if we could talk over coffee someday. I owe you an explanation—"

"Leave now or I'll call the police," Gary interrupted, overhearing our conversation and rushing to the door. He had his fists clenched and looked like he was ready to pounce.

"I don't want anything to do with you ever! You got that?" I yelled, my initial fear turning to blind hatred and rage.

I slammed the door and burst into tears, as Gary promised that he'd report him to the police to make sure that he'd never come near us again.

"Now he knows where we live, Gary! I can't hide anymore!"

"He won't be back, sweetie. You have a restraining order against him, and he knows that if he comes near you, he'll be thrown back into prison. He couldn't have known you lived here... I ordered the pizza under my name."

"I can't stay here if he knows where I live. I won't feel safe ever again," I cried.

"I'm here with you, sweetie. I won't let him hurt you ever again. Mention it to Anthony next week and see what he says."

I ran to the bathroom and threw up. This wasn't happening, not now, I thought.

• • •

The following Monday, I went for coffee with Anthony and told him about everything that happened with Jack. He insisted that I call his friend because he was a police officer and he would know what I could do to protect myself. "At the very least he can keep an eye on Jack and make sure he stays away from you," he said. Just the thought of ever seeing Jack again made my skin crawl— he stole my innocence and killed my spirit, what more could he possibly want? I still blamed myself for not recognizing who he was when I met him for the first time on the bus. How could I have missed that scar above his eyebrow and the sinister look in his eyes? Anna warned me about him, and I always had a bad feeling when I was around him. I regretted not listening to these signs. No matter how much everyone around me tried to make me feel safe, I couldn't help but wonder what he might do next.

• • •

Vicki organized a baby shower for me on Wednesday after work, and she filled her house with balloons, streamers, and decorations. It was an intimate affair, with only a few of my close friends. We had a delicious buffet, full of my favourite foods, and laughed all afternoon as we played games and opened gifts. I thought that I had opened the last one, until Vicki handed me a small box that was wrapped in white paper with a pink bow on top, its card missing. I asked who it was from, but no one claimed it. "Go on, open it! We're all curious!" Vicki said, as I reluctantly tore the paper away. I looked in the box, hiding it from the women in the room, and sitting at the bottom was a lock of Anna's hair. My heartbeat quickened as I hid it in my purse. "Well? Aren't you going to show it to us?" one of my coworkers asked. Vicki could see the concern and confusion on my face, and knew that this gift shouldn't be shared with anyone. "Okay, everyone, time for cake and coffee!" she said, clapping her hands and trying to shift their focus away from me. The rest of the shower was fun, but the whole time I couldn't help but try to figure out who had sent me that gift and why, but deep down inside I believed it must have been Anna.

Later, when Vicki asked me what was in the box, I pretended it was a gift card. I don't know why I lied to her, but sometimes I needed to, just to avoid being questioned and having to explain myself.

• • •

When I got back home later, I placed the blonde lock of hair in a box where I kept the others I had received over the years. That night, I had trouble falling asleep, and after two hours of tossing and turning, I suddenly felt a heavy weight pressing on my chest, and I couldn't move or scream for help. I looked at the doorway and saw Patch hissing at me—he could tell that something was in the room with us. In the corner, the demon stood still, surrounded by blackness that looked almost like smoke or a dense fog. My baby started kicking violently as the demon crept closer, with its long arms extended out. It grabbed a hold of my feet and tried to pull me out of bed, but I fought back as I held onto a bar that was attached to the metal headboard. I tried to call out to Gary to help me, but my voice clung to my throat and I couldn't say a word. Suddenly, from the other side of the room, there was a loud bang, and then Gaby appeared, fighting with the demon and pushing it back against the wall, before it fled from the bedroom.

"Ellen, what's going on?" Gary asked, waking up when I finally got my voice back and called out for help.

"Did you not hear any of this?"

"What are you talking about?"

"Never mind, it was probably just a bad dream."

He curled up to me and held me tight, but for the rest of the night I stayed awake, afraid that it would come back for me and my child.

• • •

When I woke up the next morning, Gary wasn't in bed, so I put on my robe and went to the kitchen to find him.

"I cooked a nice warm breakfast for you, sweetie," he said when he saw me walk in.

"I'm not that hungry, baby, sorry. I'm feeling a bit off today."

He kissed me on the forehead and then poured me a cup of coffee as I sat down at the table.

"You have to at least eat something small. If not for you, then for the baby," he said, placing a plate with some scrambled eggs and toast in front of me.

I forced myself to eat and started to feel sick as soon as I did. I was completely drained after the events of the night before and was worried about the baby and her reaction to the dark spirit. I felt alone now more than ever—all I wanted to do was talk about this with someone, but no one would believe me. Gary was convinced that I suffered from night terrors, which I suppose was his way of rationalizing the inexplicable.

• • •

When I arrived at work, Anthony was there already and seemed distant when I greeted him.

"What's eating at you this morning?" I asked.

"A lot! I have to get a case ready for court tomorrow and there's still so much work to do. I'm just feeling a bit stressed, that's all," he answered, looking like he hadn't slept the night before.

"Is there anything I can do to help?"

"It would require you to work overtime, and I don't want to ask you to do that."

"I don't mind at all! Tomorrow is my last day, so I'll help out in any way I can."

I called Gary to let him know that I probably wouldn't be home before ten that night. Anthony and I worked all day and well into the evening, eating cold pizza for dinner as we prepared for court the next day. By the time we were finally done, it was eleven and I called Gary to let him know that I was on my way home. "I couldn't have done this without you, Ellen. Thank you so much for all your help. I'm really going to miss you when you're gone," Anthony said as he shut off the lights in the office. I picked up my jacket and we left through the back door exit to the parking lot. I never liked going out there at night because it wasn't very well lit, so I asked him to walk with me to my car.

As we got closer, we jumped when we heard someone shouting, "Stop right there!" When we turned around, we saw a man running towards us with a gun in his hand. Anthony immediately stood in front of me to protect me, and as the man got closer, I began to recognize him.

"Jack?" I said, my voice cracking.

"Surprise!" he answered, with an eerie smile on his face.

I had imagined all kinds of scenarios, but this definitely wasn't one of them. I felt so helpless, and thanked God that Anthony was there to try to reason with him.

"Hey man, let's talk... just put the gun down—" Anthony said in a calm voice.

"Shut up, smartass!" Jack interrupted, tightening his grip on it.

"Jack, please put it down," I pleaded, holding onto my stomach in any effort to shield my child.

"You didn't really think that a restraining order could keep me away from you, did you?"

"Jack, what are your intentions here? Just put the gun down," Anthony said.

"I told you to shut the fuck up, man! Ellen is my girl and, if I can't have her, no one will!"

"Jack, I'm begging you, please put the gun down. Let's talk about this," I cried.

"Oh, so now you want to talk? Well it's too late for that missy," Jack answered, stepping closer.

I felt a sharp pain in my stomach and bent over.

"Something is wrong," I yelled. "My baby—"

"Why should I give a shit about your baby? It's not like it's mine! Get in my car right now, or I swear that someone is going to get shot!" Jack threatened.

I felt something warm running down my inner thighs, and when I looked down, I saw blood.

"Oh God, help me, please help me!" I screamed.

Anthony supported me as I laid down on the ground, and when I looked to my right, I saw three shadows standing next to me: Anna, Alma, and Gaby. I heard Anna say, "Fight, Ellen, you need to fight for your life." Then, Gaby put her hand on my head and said, "You will be okay, just stay strong." Next, I heard a man's voice yelling in the distance, "Hey... is everything okay over there?" I screamed out like a raving madwoman, "Call the police!" Jack was alarmed and shot the gun, and the next thing I knew, Anthony fell to the ground, covered in blood.

"Anthony? Oh my God, he's not breathing!" I cried, trying to find a pulse. "Jack, I beg you, please get some help! Can you please do this one thing for me?"

"Nah, I don't think so. Everyone says that I'm a monster, remember? Now get off him and get in my car before I shoot you too!"

"I can't... I can't stand up," I said, my voice weak and shaky.

He came closer and kicked me in the stomach, "I said... get up!" Bursts of pain shot through my entire body, and there was blood everywhere. All I could think about was how badly this was going to end. "You looked a hundred times better before you got pregnant with this little bastard," Jack said, glaring at me with pure evil in his eyes. I managed to pull myself up and tried to run away, as he yelled, "Stop, Ellen, I'm warning you—I will shoot you!"

I heard sirens—it was music to my ears—and saw a police cruiser rush into the parking lot. Jack ran to his car, turned the ignition, and tried to flee, his tires squealing. One of the officers jumped out, while the driver sped off to chase after Jack, and then an ambulance pulled in and the paramedics immediately began working on Anthony. It was too late—he didn't have a pulse. "I'm so sorry, miss, but your husband didn't make it." I thought I was having a nightmare and prayed that I would wake up and everything would be normal again. "He's not my husband," I said, crying so hard that I choked.

He's my soulmate.

I heard the first responders talk amongst each other as a woman brought me over to the ambulance so they could examine me.

"She's lost a lot of blood. We need to get her to the hospital right away." I passed out and the next thing I knew, I woke up in a hospital bed. "She's very lucky to be alive," the doctor said to a nurse, before he put a needle in my arm and placed a mask over my mouth and nose. A few seconds later, I blacked out.

* * *

Gary told me later that he got to the hospital after the police went to our house to tell him what had happened. They took him to the emergency room, where a nurse gave him a blue hospital robe, a mask, and a pair of medical gloves. He lingered anxiously, pacing back and forth in the waiting room, until the doctor finally came in. He took Gary to a private room and informed him that I had lost a lot of blood, and they had to perform a caesarian to save the baby.

He stayed in the emergency room overnight, and then in the morning, a nurse tapped him on the shoulder and told him that he could see me, and as soon as he walked into my room, we both burst into tears.

"My sweetheart, I am so sorry I wasn't there to protect you," he said, holding my hand.

"Anthony's dead, Gary," I said bluntly.

"The policeman told me. I am so, so sorry, sweetie."

"Jack… what happened to him? I hope they shot him!"

"I heard on the news this morning that they captured him, and he's back in prison."

"This is all my fault. If I hadn't asked Anthony to walk me to my car, he might still be alive."

"Don't blame yourself for this, Ellen. Jack is the criminal here, not you."

"Have you seen the baby?" I asked.

"Yes, we have a daughter, and she is just as beautiful as you," he answered, kissing my forehead.

"It's a girl? I want to see her!"

Gary asked the nurse to bring in our baby girl, and when she did, she placed her on my stomach. My emotions were all over the place, I cried because of my grief for what happened to Anthony, but at the same time, I was overcome with joy because my daughter was healthy and safe. Gary left the room to get a warm blanket and, while he was out, I looked at her, examining her chubby cheeks and counting her little fingers and toes. She weighed seven pounds and, even though the nurse assured me that was a good size for a newborn, I was still afraid to break her as I held her in my arms. She had my eyes and Gary's full lips and thick hair. She started kicking her legs in a jagged motion before curling her tiny fingers around my pinky. My heart was full, and I couldn't help but wonder if she would be able to communicate with the dead like her mother. Then, when I rubbed my hand over her shoulders, I noticed some redness, and as I looked closer I saw a birth mark in the shape of a butterfly. I had goosebumps all over—now she would be protected just like I had been for so long. I looked to my left and saw Anna standing in the corner of my room, and we smiled at each other. "Anna, meet Anna," I said, as I raised the baby up. I saw tears in my best friend's eyes, and then she vanished.

I couldn't remember what happened between the time the ambulance took me to the hospital and when I woke up from the surgery. The only thing I recalled was having a dream about a little boy being born, it felt so real that I thought it was my own baby, but how could that be? Gaby and Anna had told me that it was a girl. Vicki's cries jolted me out of my contemplation, as she rushed into the room and kissed me on the forehead. "She's so beautiful, Ellen," she said, her eyes watering, as she looked at baby Anna, who was sleeping in a little hospital cot that was placed next to my bed. She said that, when she heard what Jack did, she prayed for me and the baby, even though praying wasn't her thing—but it seemed to work. Vicki had this glow about her, her smile and eyes were lighting up the room.

She took my hand and said, "I have something to tell you, Ellen." Whatever it was, it had to be big news because I had never felt so much love and joy around her as I did in that instant. "Robert and

I received a call from the adoption agency. We're having a baby, Ellen!" My heart melted—could this day get any better? She went on to say that the baby was born to a girl, who was only seventeen and too young to take on the responsibilities of motherhood. Vicki said that the baby would be coming home later that week. This was so surreal. I realized that the baby was born on the same day as my daughter—I had experienced too much to write this off as a coincidence. "Vicki, it's a little boy... isn't it?" She looked at me with wide eyes. "How do you know that?" she asked. "I just do," I answered.

"Ellen, there's something else—" she continued, as I held my breath, anticipating what she would say next. "If you're okay with it, I would like to name him Anthony. I know how much he meant to you and the connection you two had was so special. What do you think?" I couldn't believe that this was happening. Not only was her adoptive son and my daughter born on the same day, but this was also the same day that Anthony died—would they be soulmates too? "Oh, Vicki, you have no idea how happy this makes me," I said, as I held her hands. "Of course, I'm okay with it!" We hugged and cried in each other's arms—this was by far the best day of our lives.

• • •

That night, I dreamt about the white tunnel and saw seven people sitting at a table again. This time, I recognized all of them. They smiled at me and waved goodbye, like this was the last time I'd see them. The next day, I was released from the hospital. Before I arrived home with the baby, Gary had taken Patch back to the animal shelter, and they found a home for him that same day. That made me happy, he deserved to live a normal life, and so did I. As soon as I walked through the door, I immediately went upstairs to look inside the box where I kept Anna's locks of hair, and it was empty. I felt like a part of my life had been erased, but maybe it was better this way. It was time for a fresh start.

No one knows what the future holds, but sometimes it can grant you new beginnings.

. . .

That following September, I took seven roses with me to the cemetery. After I placed two red roses on my parent's graves, I walked over to Anna's and laid down the other five. A pink rose for Anna, two red roses for her mother and Gaby, a blue rose for Anthony, and a white rose for Alma. Even though Anthony, his mother, and Gaby were not buried there, I knew that their spirits were joined to Anna's, and that's what mattered.

When I left the cemetery, a swarm of seven fluttering butterflies followed me to my car, and I felt at peace for the first time in my life.

Goodbye butterflies. I will forever be grateful to you, my angels.

THE END

ACKNOWLEDGEMENTS

Thank you to my wonderful son, Patrick, for your unconditional love and for the joy you bring to my life. You rock my world!

I would also like to thank my friend and Muse, Peggy McColl. Your continual words of encouragement and your strong belief in my abilities helped me write this book after pondering it for so long.

A special thank you to my amazing editor, Michelle Sugar. Your extensive grasp of the story and its characters, as well as your respect for my writing style, made my words shine.

Finally, I would like to express my gratitude to the amazing team at Hasmark Publishing for making my publishing dream come true—I could not have done this without your help.

ABOUT THE AUTHOR

Louise L. Tremblay lives in beautiful Ottawa, Canada, where she enjoys spending time with her son, family, and friends. As a business executive, she has enjoyed a successful career in communications, high-tech, and business intelligence. She is passionate about writing and is excited to share her remarkable story in her debut novel, which is inspired by some of her own experiences.

Hearts to be Heard

Giving a Voice to Creativity!

With every donation, a voice will be given to
the creativity that lies within the hearts of
our children living with diverse challenges.

By making this difference, children that may
not have been given the opportunity to have their
Heart Heard will have the freedom to create
beautiful works of art and musical creations.

Donate by visiting
HeartstobeHeard.com

We thank you.

Manufactured by Amazon.ca
Bolton, ON

13795430R00120